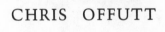

CHRIS OFFUTT

KENTUCKY STRAIGHT

Chris Offutt is the author of *Out of the Woods*, *The Same River Twice*, and *The Good Brother*. All have been translated into several languages. His work is widely anthologized and has received many honors, including a Guggenheim Fellowship and a Whiting Award. He lives in Iowa City with his wife and sons.

KENTUCKY STRAIGHT

KENTUCKY

STRAIGHT

CHRIS OFFUTT

VINTAGE CONTEMPORARIES

VINTAGE BOOKS

A DIVISION OF RANDOM HOUSE, INC.

NEW YORK

A VINTAGE CONTEMPORARIES ORIGINAL, NOVEMBER 1992
FIRST EDITION

Some of these stories appeared in slightly different form in *Ploughshares, Michigan Quarterly Review, Willow Springs, Northwest Review, High Plains Literary Review, Quarterly West,* and *Coe Review.*

The verse from "Another Place," from *The Late Hour,* is reprinted from *Selected Poems* by Mark Strand, by permission of Alfred A. Knopf, Inc.

Library of Congress Cataloging-in-Publication Data
Offutt, Chris.
Kentucky straight / Chris Offutt. — 1st ed.
p. cm. — (Vintage contemporaries)
ISBN 0-679-73886-X (pbk.)
1. Kentucky—Fiction. I. Title.
PS3565.F387K4 1992
813'.54—dc20 91-58062
CIP

BOOK DESIGN BY CATHRYN S. AISON
MAP COPYRIGHT © 1992 BY JAYE ZIMET

Author photo © Sandy Dyas

Manufactured in the United States of America
13579B8642

For Rita

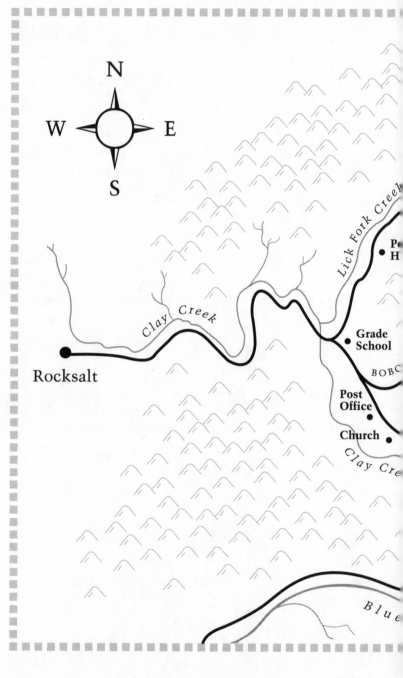

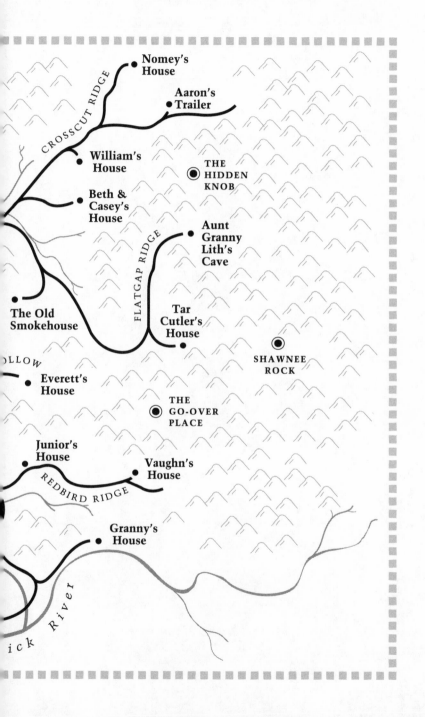

The author wishes to thank Jane O. Burns,
the Copernicus Society of America
for its James A. Michener Grant,
and the Kentucky Arts Council.

this is the mirror
in which pain is asleep
this is the country
nobody visits
    —Mark Strand
    "Another Place"

CONTENTS

KENTUCKY

STRAIGHT

SAWDUST

Not a one on this hillside finished high school. Around here a man is judged by how he acts, not how smart he's supposed to be. I don't hunt, fish, or work. Neighbors say I think too much. They say I'm like my father and Mom worries that maybe they're right.

When I was a kid we had a coonhound that got into a skunk, then had the gall to sneak under the porch. He whimpered in the dark and wouldn't come out. Dad shot him. It didn't stink less but Dad felt better. He told Mom that any dog who didn't know coon from skunk ought to be killed.

"He's still back under the porch," Mom said.

"I know it," Dad said. "I loved Tater, too. I don't reckon I could stand to bury him."

He looked at my brother and me.

"Don't you even think of putting them boys under that porch," Mom yelled. "It's your dog. You get it."

She held her nose and walked around the house. Dad looked at us again. "You boys smell anything?"

My eyes were watered up but I shook my head no.

"Dead things stink," said Warren.

"So does a wife sometimes," Dad said, handing me his rifle. "Here, Junior. Put this up and fetch my rod and reel."

I ran into the house for his fishing pole. When I got outside, Dad was on his knees shining a flashlight under the porch. Back in the corner lay old Tater, dead as a mallet. "Blind casting," Dad said. "This might turn out fun."

He spread his legs and whipped the rod and the line went humming under the porch. He reeled in a piece of rag. Dad threw again and hooked Tater but only pulled out a hunk of fur. On the next cast, his line got hung. He jerked hard on the fishing pole. The line snapped, the rod lashed over his shoulder and hit Warren in the face. Mom came running around the house at Warren's screams.

"What'd you do now?" she said.

"Line broke," Dad said. "Eight-pound test. Lost a good split sinker, too."

"Why don't you cut a hole in the floor and fish him out like an ice pond!"

"Don't know where my saw's at."

"That's the worst of it! You'd have gone and done it."

She towed Warren up the gray board steps into the house. Dad broke the fishing pole across his knee. "Never should have had no kids," he said, and threw the ruined rod over the hill. A jaybird squalled into the sky. Dad grabbed my shoulders and leaned his face to mine.

"I wanted to be a horse doctor," he said, "but you know what?"

I shook my head. His fingers dug me deep.

"I quit sixth grade on account of not having nothing to wear. All my kin did. Every last one of us."

He turned loose of me and I watched his bowed back fade into the trees. Wide leaves of poplar rustled behind him.

A few years later Dad gave his gun away and joined the church. He got Warren a pup that fell off the porch and broke its leg. Dad cried all day. I was scared, but Mom said his crying was a sign that both his oars were back in the water. She told me to be proud. That Sunday, Dad climbed on top of a church pew in the middle of service. I thought he'd felt the Lord's touch and would start talking in tongues. The preacher stopped his sermon. Dad looked around the room and swore to high heaven he would heal our pup's busted leg or die trying. Mom made him sit down and hush. I got scared again.

After church Dad carried the pup out the ridge to a hickory where he tried all day to fix its leg. He was still yelling at God when Mom sent us to bed. She found Dad in the morning. He'd taken off his belt and hanged himself. On the ground below him lay the pup, all its legs broken. It was still alive.

Warren and I both quit school. He got a job and saved his money. I took to the woods hunting mushrooms, ginseng, and mayapple root. I've been places a rabbit wouldn't go.

Last fall Warren pushed a trailer up a hollow and moved into it. He said the one thing I was good for was taking care of Mom. Twice a week I walked to the Clay Creek Post Office at the foot of the hill. It and the church was all we had and they sat side by side between the creek and the road. Most people went to both but Mom and I divided it up. I got more mail than her and she took enough gospel for the whole county. I subscribed to a peck of magazines and read everything twice, even letters and household hints. They stopped coming because I never paid.

Some days I went to the post office early to look at crooks the government wants. Sixty photographs were stapled together like a feed store calendar, and the faces were just regular folks. Under each one was a list of what the person did, where his scars were, and if he was black or white. It seemed odd to show a picture of a man and say what color he was. Around here, we're mostly brown. I wouldn't mind talking to somebody of another color but they don't ever come around these parts. Nobody does. This is a place people move away from.

One afternoon I saw a sign in the post office about a GED. Anyone could take the high school test from a VISTA center in town, and that set me to thinking on what Dad said about quitting school. He never read anything but the King James Bible and about a hundred maps. Dad collected maps the way some men kept dogs—big maps and little maps, favorites and no-counts. I've seen him study maps over a tree stump till way past dark. He wanted to know where the Land of Nod was at and who all lived there. The preacher told him it was lost in the Flood. Dad didn't think so.

"Everywhere has to be somewhere," he always said.

The GED fretted me for two days' worth of walking in the woods. I almost stepped on a blue racer sunning on a rock. We watched each other for a spell, him shooting a little forked tongue out and me not able to think of nothing but taking that test. Most people run from a snake without ever knowing if it was poison or just alive. The GED was the same way. Failing couldn't hurt me, and getting it would make everybody on the hill know I wasn't what they thought. Maybe then they'd think about Dad differently, too.

The next morning I hitchhiked to Rocksalt and stood on the sidewalk. People stared from cars. My hand was on the test place doorknob and sweat poured off me. I opened the door. The air was cool and the walls were white. Behind a metal desk sat a lady painting her fingernails pink. She looked at me, then at her nails.

"The barbershop is next door," she said.

"I don't want a haircut, ma'am. I might could use one but that ain't what I come to town for."

"It ain't," she said like she was mocking me. She talked fast and didn't always say her words right. I wondered what brought her to the hills. Things must be getting pretty bad if city people were coming here for work.

"I'll take that GED," I said.

"Who sent you?"

"Nobody."

She stared at me a long time. Her hand moved like she was waving away flies and when the nail polish was dry, she opened a drawer and gave me a study book. It was magazine size with a black plastic binder.

"Come back when you're ready," she said. "I'm here to help you people."

I was five hours getting home and the heat didn't bother me a bit. By the time I got to the house, somebody had seen me in town and told a neighbor, who told Mom at the prayer meeting. That's the way it is around here. A man can sneeze and it'll beat him back to the porch.

"They say you're fixing to get learned up on us," she said. "You might read the Bible while you're at it."

"I done did. Twice."

"I ain't raised no heathen then."

After supper I hit those practice tests. My best was reading and worst was math. A man can take a mess of figures and make it equal out to something different. Maybe some people like math for that, but a pile of stove wood doesn't equal a tree. It made me wonder where the sawdust went to in a math problem. After all that ciphering, there wasn't anything to show for the work, nothing to clean up, nothing to look at. A string of numbers was like an owl pellet lying in a game path. You knew a bird had flew over, but not the direction.

Warren pulled his four-wheel-drive pickup into the yard, honking the horn. He used to work in town until they built a car plant in Lexington. Now he drives three hours a day to work and back. He's got a video dish, a microwave, and a VCR.

His boots hit the porch and the front door slammed. He walked in our old room. "What do you know, Junior? All on your ownself and afraid to tell it."

I shook my head. After Dad died, Warren went all out to make people like him. I went the other way.

"Hear you're eat up with the smart bug," he said. "And taking that school test in town."

"Thinking on it."

"You ought to let up on that and try working. Then you can wear alligator-hide boots like these."

He pulled a pants leg up.

"Where'd you get them from?" I said.

"Down to Lex. They got a mall big as two pastures laid end to end. I bought these boots right out of the window. Paid the man cash, too."

"He saw you coming, Warren. They ain't made no alligator nothing in nigh ten years. Government's got them took care of."

"What makes you know so much?"

"Read it in a magazine."

Warren frowned. He doesn't put much store in anything but TV. Commercials are real people to him. I knew he was getting mad by a neck vein that popped up big as a night crawler.

"I ought to kick your butt with these boots," he said.

"That won't make them gator."

"It won't take the new out either." He scuffed my workshoes that were ordered from the Sears and Roebuck catalog. "You're still wearing them goddam Wishbook clod-hoppers."

"Warren!" Mom screeched from the kitchen.

She doesn't mind cussing too awful much but taking the Lord's name in vain is one thing she won't stand for. Dad used to do it just to spite her.

"You know what GED stands for?" Warren said. "Get Even Dumber."

He stomped outside, started his truck, and rammed it through the gears. Road dust rose thick as smoke behind him. I watched the moon haul itself above Redbird Ridge. Night crawled up the hollow. I went outside and sat on Dad's old map-stump. A long time ago I was scared of the dark until Dad told me it was the same as day, only the air was a different color.

In a week I'd taken every practice test twice and was ready for the real one. Everybody on the hill knew what I was doing. The preacher guaranteed Mom a sweet place in heaven for all her burdens on earth. He said I was too hardheaded for my own good.

I got to thinking about that in the woods and decided maybe it wasn't a bad thing to be. I'm not one to pick wildflowers and bring them inside where they'll die quicker. And I'll not cut down a summer shade tree to burn for winter firewood. Taking the GED was the first time I'd ever been stubborn over the doing of something, instead of the not doing. Right there's where Dad and me were different. He was hardheaded over things he never had a say in.

In the morning I left the hill and walked halfway to town before getting a ride that dropped me off at the test place. The lady was surprised to see me. She wrote my name on a form, and asked for fifteen dollars to take the test. I didn't say anything.

"Do you have the fee?" she asked.

"No."

"Do you have a job?"

"No."

"Do you live with family?"

"Mom."

"Does she have a job?"

"No."

"Do you receive welfare assistance?"

"No, ma'am."

"Then how do you and your mother get along?"

"We don't talk much."

She tightened her mouth and shook her head. Her voice came slow and loud, like I was deaf.

"What do you and your mother do for money?"

"Never had much need for it."

"What about food?"

"We grow it."

The lady set her pencil down and leaned away from the desk. On the wall behind her hung a picture of the governor wearing a tie. I looked through the window at the hardware store across the street. Dad died owing it half on a new chain saw. We got a bill after the funeral and Mom sold a quilt her great-aunt made, to pay the debt.

I was thinking hard and not getting far. There wasn't

anything I had to sell. Warren would give me the money but I could never ask him for it. I turned to leave.

"Junior," said the lady. "You can take the test anyway."

"I don't need the help."

"It's free when you're living in poverty."

"I'll owe you," I said. "Pay you before the first snow."

She led me through a door to a small room with no windows. I squeezed into a school desk and she gave me four yellow pencils and the test. When I finished, she said to come back in a month and see if I passed. She told me in a soft voice that I could take the test as many times as necessary. I nodded and headed out of town toward home. I couldn't think or feel. I was doing good to walk.

Every night Mom claimed a worry that I was getting above my raisings. Warren wouldn't talk to me at all. I wandered the hills, thinking of what I knew about the woods. I can name a bird by its nest and a tree by the bark. A cucumber smell means a copperhead's close. The sweetest blackberries are low to the ground and locust makes the best fence post. It struck me funny that I had to take a test to learn I was living in poverty. I'd say the knowing of it is what drove Dad off his feed for good. When he died, Mom burned his maps but I saved the one of Kentucky. Where we live wasn't on it.

I stayed in the woods three weeks straight. When I finally went to the post office, the mail hadn't run yet. It was the first of the month and a lot of people were waiting on government checks. The oldest sat inside, out of the sun, and the rest of us stood in willow shade by the creek. A Monroe boy jabbed his brother and pointed at me.

"If it ain't the doctor," he said, "taking a break off his books."

"Hey, Doctor, you aiming to get smart and rich?"

"Yeah," said his brother. "He's going to start a whorehouse and run it by hand."

Everybody laughed, even a couple of old women with hair buns like split pine cones. I decided to skip the mail and go home. Then the one boy made me mad.

"I got a sick pup at the house, Doctor. You as good on them as your daddy was?"

Way it is around here, I had to do more than just fight. Sometimes a man will lay back a year before shooting somebody's dog to get back at its owner, but with everyone watching, I couldn't just leave. I walked to their pickup and kicked out a headlight. The youngest Monroe came running but I tripped him and he rolled in the dirt. The other one jumped on my back, tearing at my ear with his teeth. His legs had a hold I couldn't break. He kept hitting the side of my face. I fell backwards on the truck hood and he let go of me then. Two old men held back the other boy. I crossed the creek and climbed the steep hill home, spitting blood all the way.

Mom never said a word after she heard what the fight was over. Warren came by the next night.

"I got one at the creek and the other at the head of Bobcat Holler," he said. "They'll not talk that way no more."

"Whip them pretty bad?"

"They knowed they was in a fight."

Warren'd taken a lick or two in the jaw, and his neck vein was puffed out again. A railroad tie won't knock him over.

"You still getting that GED?" he said.

"Friday."

"I'm getting me a TV that runs on batteries."

"What for?"

"To sit and look at."

"Same with me, Warren. Same with me."

He pushed his fingers at a swollen place below his cheekbone. His shoulders sagged. "I'll fight for you, Junior. And for Daddy, too. But I never could figure what either of you ever was up to."

He went outside and opened the truck door with his thumbs. The knuckles of both hands were split, and bending his fingers would open the scabs. One was already leaking a little. He started the truck in second gear so he wouldn't have to shift, and drove away with his palms. I watched him till the dust settled back to the road.

On Friday I walked the ridgeline above the creek all the way to town. Rocksalt lay in a wide bottom between the hills. I'd never seen it from above and it looked pretty small, nothing to be afraid of. I went down the slope, crossed the creek, and stepped onto the sidewalk. For a long time I stood in front of the test center. I could leave now and never know if I passed or flunked. Either one scared me. I opened the door and looked in.

"Congratulations," said the lady.

She handed me a state certificate saying I'd achieved

a high school degree. My name was written in black ink. Below it was a gold seal and the governor's signature.

"I have a job application for you," she said. "It isn't a promise of work but you qualify now. Employment is the next step out."

"All I wanted was this."

"Not a job?"

"No, ma'am."

She sighed and looked down, rubbing her eyes. She leaned against the doorjamb. "Sometimes I don't know what I'm doing here," she said.

"None of us do," I said. "Most people around here are just waiting to die."

"That's not funny, Junior."

"No, but what's funny is, everybody gets up awful early anyhow."

"I like to sleep late," she said.

She was still smiling when I shut the door behind me. I'd come as close as a man could get to finishing school and it didn't feel half bad. At the edge of town I looked back at the row of two-story buildings. Dad used to say a smart man wouldn't bother with town, but now I knew he was wrong. Anybody can go there any time. Town's just a bunch of people living together in the only wide place between the hills.

I left the road and walked through horseweed to the creek bank. It was a good way to find pop bottles and I still owed the state fifteen dollars.

HOUSE RAISING

Rain chewed fresh gullies in the ridge road, turning the hard clay dirt to a yellow paste. The ditch overflowed and gray air blurred the low horizon. Dripping leaves hung limp and heavy.

"It'll pass," Mercer said.

Coe lit a cigarette and opened the pickup window an inch. Pellets of rain spattered his shoulder. The top of the windshield was breath-fogged from an hour of waiting and watching the rain. The truck cab smelled dog wet.

"Hope how soon that dozer comes," Mercer said. "You?"

Coe didn't answer. Finger marks of mud streaked the

brim of his cap. He was from out of the county, where Mercer's brother had bought a used mobile home. Earlier that morning, Coe and his boss had the trailer hauled halfway up the slope when rain turned the fresh-cleared earth to swamp. The trailer sank past the axles. The tow truck buried its rear tires, trying to pull the trailer free. Neighbor men who'd come to watch laughed and laughed. They were waiting for the wet earth to pitch the trailer down the hill into the creek. Maybe the tow truck would follow, like a bluetick chained to a dog box. The men would wait all day for that. It was worth the rain and chill.

"This ain't bad, " Mercer said. "Setting in a truck for pay. How long you had this job?"

"Three months."

"Like it?"

"No."

"If it was me, I'd like it," Mercer said. "How come you don't?"

Shifting wind drilled water against the roof. Coe tossed his cigarette out the window, where rain slammed it down and gutted it. Coe watched the tobacco and paper vanish, wondering how people could live on vertical land. No sky. No river. Nothing but shacks, mud, and woods so dense Coe couldn't see past the tree line. The midday air was dark as dusk. He'd heard that every hillbilly had one leg shorter than the other from years of walking on the slant.

"Before this," Coe said, "had me a job six years on a horse farm."

"Good work if you can get it."

"Not too awful bad. Helped the vet till my wife's

cousin died. Told the big boss I was going to the funeral and he said not to come back."

"First cousin?"

Coe nodded.

"What'd you do?"

"Went."

"Got to stand by family," Mercer said. "Man like that ain't worth working for."

"No," Coe said. He twisted against the truck door to face Mercer full on. "But some people don't like niggers."

Mercer leaned forward, squinting, head cocked.

"Hear that dozer," he said. "Halfway up the hill, my opinion." He looked at the water drenching the land. "Some people don't like nothing."

Two rain-dark figures rode the rumbling bulldozer to the top of the hill; Coe waved it out the ridge and followed in the truck. The dozer punched black smoke into the mist as it stopped beside an old hickory. Several men squatted beneath the tree, their arms extended, elbows propped on bony knees. They waited in the rain as if it was sun, oblivious to the wet and the cold. Water glazed their faces to a uniform mask.

Only Mercer's brother stood. Aaron weighed three hundred pounds and was freshly married. For two weeks Mercer had helped him clear a narrow strip of Crosscut Ridge for Aaron's new home. They widened a game path to a road and chain-sawed trees to stovewood chunks. They plowed a trailer-size notch into the hill, and buried a culvert for draining sewage to the creek. Jagged teeth of limestone protruded from the stripped land.

Mercer slammed the pickup door and walked

through the dim fog. The men watched, wondering what Mercer had learned in the truck. They'd never ask but would wait instead, wait a month or a year until Mercer brought it up himself. Then they'd hear the truth, not a story tainted by the asking.

Mercer jerked his head to the bulldozer. "Old Bob's here."

"Late," his brother said. He unleashed a stream of tobacco juice that dissipated rapidly in the rain. "He best not be too bad off."

"You know he is," said one of the men, unfolding upward from his squat. "Old Bob gets so drunk he takes back things he never stole."

Everyone grinned and the man repeated himself, drawing another round of headshakes and laughter. Eight years before, these same men dug Old Bob out of a caved-in mine a mile away. In one hand he held a long splinter of strut wood he'd yanked from his face. Its sharp end spindled his eyeball. The company gave him a bulldozer with a loose track and three cylinders that didn't hit. After the mines were empty and the company gone, Old Bob owned the only dozer in the hills. A good swap, people said. He'd traded up.

Old Bob staggered through the mud, bandy-legged from a decade's habit of staying upright while drunk. He jerked his head like a crow to see with his one good eye.

"Hidy, by God! Think it'll rain?"

"Don't know," said a man. "But it sure missed a good chance to if it don't."

Aaron used a blunt finger to search behind his jaw for strings of tobacco. He flung them to the ground and slipped a fresh chew in his mouth.

"Reckon you can pull her out?" he said.

Old Bob stared at the trailer jammed in the mud of the wet clay slope. A heavy chain ran to the tow truck. It was mired deep as the trailer. The truck driver lowered himself from the cab, holding tightly to the door. He slipped on the soap-slick ground and fell, skidding sideways down the hill. He plunged to his knees in the rushing water of the ditch.

"Look out, boys," Old Bob said. "He's a-looking for a dance partner."

The driver forced a grin as he slogged across the road.

"I'm Mr. Richards," he said. "You the dozer man?"

"Ain't needing one, are you?"

"Might could."

Old Bob leaned forward and twitched his head. Strands of shiny wet hair clung to his face in diagonal strips. He peeled one back and sucked its tip.

"Richards," he said. "Same as Dick, ain't it. You the boss of this here outfit?"

Old Bob howled, his clothes flapping like birch bark flayed by wind. The men hid sly grins, looking up the hill or at their boots, having learned from the mines never to anger a foreman.

Richards breathed through his mouth to keep rain from his nose. Only white people bought new mobile homes, trading an old one for down payment. Richards was running out of blacks to buy his used trailers. The hill people were his next market and he had to be careful.

"They say you work a dozer like a borrowed mule," Richards said. "Ready to hit a lick?"

Old Bob poked out his lower lip and shook his head.

"Not yet, I ain't. Got to get myself lubed a little more." He reeled to face the bulldozer. A man-shape hanging within the roll cage rocked and swayed. "Hey, Bobby, toss me that bottle here!" Old Bob grinned at the men and focused his single eye on Mr. Richards.

"My boy was born lamed-up but his eyes are good. He's the one does the seeing for me. I'd say Dick here could use a boy walking for him, way he come off that hillside."

Old Bob showed his teeth and strutted to the bulldozer. The men followed, eager for heat against the hissing rain. Richards kicked mud from his boot.

"Where's Coe at?" he said. "Hey, Coe!"

"In the truck," Mercer said. "I'll get him."

Mercer walked past the men sharing whiskey and damp cigarettes cupped in palms. The bulldozer clattered on idle. "Save me a taste," he said to the men.

Coe rolled the window down, releasing cigarette smoke that faded into the fog. Mercer wondered why he stayed alone in the truck. A man only did that if he was trying to avoid a fight, but Coe worked hard and didn't say much.

"Boss man's wanting you," Mercer said.

"Don't that figure. Him and that dozer feller get into it already?"

"Old Bob's half drunk is all."

"I wouldn't mind that," Coe said. "I could stand a snort myself, day like this."

"Might not be none left."

"Not for me, anyhow." He rolled up his window and left the truck. "Rain ain't let up a hair."

"No," Mercer said. "But it's only water."

Mud sucked at their boots beneath the dark tunnel of tree limbs. The wind had stilled. Rain dropped straight from the sky as if following ropes to the earth. When Mercer and Coe passed the bulldozer, the men hushed and stared. Coe scuttled sideways up the muddy slope.

The bank's lower section had slid a few feet to block the ditch. Backwash flowed across the road, cutting new troughs to the creek below, and Mercer knew the bank might not hold past dark. One of the men passed Mercer the pint. With three fingers lost to a chain saw, the man's hand made a C-clamp around the flat bottle. An inch of corn liquor sloshed the bottom.

Old Bob settled onto the bulldozer's seat. Behind him, propped in the roll cage with crippled legs dangling, was his son Bobby—Bobby the Finder. He could spot a snake fifty yards away and label birds above the farthest ridge. In spring, Old Bob carried him like a sack of feed corn while Bobby's forked dowsing rod jumped and quivered. Of twenty-seven wells dug where Bobby said, twenty-five hit underground springs. Everyone blamed Old Bob for the two mistakes. He was drunk and didn't walk straight.

The dozer rattled up the slope, steel tracks flipping bricks of mud. Rainwater rushed to fill the ladder-shaped prints. Bobby hung like a scarecrow, yelling directions. The dozer moved easily over the mud as Old Bob maneuvered it to the truck. Coe fastened a tow chain to the bulldozer's hitch. Richards gunned the truck, spattering mud. The chain rose taut and the bulldozer reared like a cornered bear until Old Bob released the tension. The machine slammed back to earth, spraying Coe with a sheet of yellow mud. The dozer tugged again, and the truck's twin rear wheels spun. Each abrupt motion jerked Bobby hanging from the roll bar. The straining truck suddenly jumped up the hillside and rain gushed into the hole. Clay dirt held it like a bowl. The men watched mud float in the yellow water.

Old Bob dragged the truck in a tight circle. He saluted the men in the road, who punched each other's soggy arms. Richards leaned from the truck window, his mouth raging in a shout that was lost to the sound of dozer and rain. Old Bob made another pass of the narrow ridge and in a final sharp turn, he whipped the truck sideways, slinging great waves of mud into its open window. The tow truck stalled. Old Bob cut the bulldozer to a rumbling throb and waved at the men. The wet woods were black behind him. He sat alone on the rattling dozer.

"Where's Bobby?" Mercer said.

"Ain't he up there?" said a man.

"Well, he ain't gone far," said another. "Grandmaw can outrun him and she's dead."

The men watched Richards wave his hands and point to the rear of the truck. Old Bob eased to the muddy ground.

"Never seen him off that dozer on a job," someone said. "Track probably come off."

The men crossed the road to climb the hill. Aaron waited behind, spitting over his shoulder. This was his land and his trailer. He would stay clear of mud.

Cold rain streamed Mercer's face as he climbed a grassy bank untouched by plow or dozer. He circled the mud-flecked trailer, staying on the high furrow between tire tracks. Coe stood at the trailer's corner, head raised to a waterfall pouring off the roof. He wiped mud from his face.

"You aiming to shave next?" Mercer said.

Coe stiffened. He stepped forward, anger fading as he saw the offered whiskey.

"Save me some," Mercer said, and tossed the bottle.

Coe caught it, uncapped the pint, and took a quick pull. He closed his eyes at the cool burn.

"That dozer man's dumb as dirt," he said.

"Boy of his is all right," Mercer said. "Can't say how he got that way, but he did."

"The son don't have to be the pa."

"Around here, he mostly is."

"You people got it bad as us."

"Maybe," Mercer said. "I never knowed nobody else."

They looked away from each other as raindrops pocked the mud. Coe stared into the mist, thinking that he'd been wrong, that these people had it worse. Coe knew how black folks were. He knew how they got that way, and who to blame. The hillbillies didn't.

They stood without speaking until Coe saw the men appear in the fog and approach the tow truck.

"Something done went wrong," Coe said.

They crossed the mud to the men squatting around the truck's rear end. Bobby lay on his back, legs pinned beneath the truck's doubled tires. His eyes were wide and he was shivering. Rain pooled in the creases of his clothes.

"You hurt bad?" Old Bob asked.

"Can't tell," Bobby said. "Never did feel nothing

down there." He coughed and a red bubble formed at his mouth. "Get me up."

"Swing that dozer around," Richards said to Old Bob. "If I drive, the tires will spin on him. You've got to haul that truck off nice and slow." His voice lowered. "No more tricks, you damn fool."

Old Bob stumbled to the bulldozer, slowed by the weight of mud on his boots. He turned and yelled. "Hey, by God, where's that whiskey?"

Coe held the bottle up.

"Hell with it," Old Bob said.

"Suits me," said Mercer.

He yanked the bottle from Coe's hand and drained the last of the clear liquor. The men stared, surprised that Mercer would drink after Coe.

The tow truck lurched a few yards, dappling everyone with mud. Bobby's ruined knee spurted a red arc. Then another. And another. The men watched, bewildered and afraid. They had slaughtered hogs in autumn and field-dressed deer in the woods. They'd seen mangled men dragged from the mines—crushed, turned blue from lack of oxygen, charred by a shaft fire. But none had watched a man slowly die.

"Goddam it," Old Bob yelled. He jumped from the bulldozer. "That's my goddam boy!"

He knelt and grabbed Bobby's knee. The severed leg slid away. It bobbed in the hole where Bobby lay, and turned the water pink. A long sharp rim of rock jutted from the mud below Bobby's stump.

"We got to do something!" Old Bob said. His eyehole held a thumb-sized wedge of clay.

"Not much a body can do," said a man.

"Tourniquet won't do no good," said another.

The rest nodded around him. They'd all lost kin; it couldn't be helped. Coe shouldered through the men and knelt in the mud. He pressed his hand against the open wound.

"We need a rope or piece of harness," Coe said. "I worked alongside a horse doc nigh six year."

Old Bob knocked Coe's arm away. "Reach for him again and you'll draw back a nub!"

Blood spouted the air twice before Coe stopped it with his palm. His other hand held Old Bob back.

"Watch what you're doing there," said one of the men. His voice was low and hard and the others moved to him. They waited in the cold gray rain, ready to back the man they knew.

Bobby leaned forward and saw the space where his leg should be. He fell back laughing a high-pitched cry. "Chop off the other one," he said. "I don't need them either one."

The men glanced at each other, avoiding Coe's impassive face. One by one they settled their patient gaze on Mr. Richards. He was the boss, he would tell them what to do. Richards blew rain from his lips.

"He did work on a horse farm," he said. "But I can't say what all he knows."

The men rubbed their mouths and adjusted their hats. Each had a firm opinion but giving an order would mark him as uppity. They stared at Bobby, their sweat mixing with rain.

Mercer removed the snakeskin belt his father had

made. He jingled the buckle. Everyone studied Mercer and the belt he held.

Slowly, carefully to ensure that the rest agreed, they began nodding to one another. They looked at Coe's hands and waited. He did nothing until a man spoke, head turned to Mercer.

"Won't hurt Bobby no worse to try," the man said. "Better take hold of Old Bob first."

Richards pulled him away. Old Bob released his son easily, too easily, and Mercer realized he had fainted. Richards laid him in the flowing silty mud.

Coe looped the belt twice on Bobby's thigh and threaded the buckle very tight. He pinched the exposed artery, tilted sideways, and pulled a knife from his pocket.

"Somebody open this," he said.

The men looked at Mercer. He took the knife, yanked the blade out, and passed it back. Coe cut Bobby's pants and folded the flaps of cloth aside. He sliced the withered leg from knee to midthigh and gently tugged six inches of artery from the slit. Twice it slipped from his hands like a tiny, wriggling snake. Blood soaked into the earth. Coe squeezed the artery, looped a knot in its end, and lifted his hands away. The blood flow strained against the knot, leaking to the mud. Coe pulled the end tighter and the bleeding stopped. The artery bulged dark against the pale knot. Coe placed his cap over the stump.

"Get him to the truck," he said.

The men moved to Bobby as if he had four corners. Coe cradled his head. They lifted him and began moving slowly down the muddy slope. Mercer watched until they faded into fog rising from the hollow's warmth. At his feet Coe's knife lay half-buried in the mud. Mercer cleaned the blade against his pants and slipped it in his pocket.

Mr. Richards crouched behind Old Bob and shook him awake. Dark rain trickled from his eye socket. Richards raised him to his feet and turned to Mercer.

"Reckon we ought not leave that leg laying out here," he said. "Dogs might get it, or something."

Air in the boot made it float on the puddle's surface. Mercer lifted it by the heel, holding the leg away from his body. It didn't weigh much. He carried it down the hill, wondering what to do with it.

His brother stood alone in the road. Rain poured from Aaron's belly like a gutterless roof.

"Where'd they all go?" Mercer said.

"Took Bobby to the doctor."

"Coe, too?"

"Who?"

"Feller driving the pickup."

"You mean the nigger?"

"No," said Mercer. "That's not who I mean, you son of a bitch."

He held Bobby's leg like a weapon. Aaron frowned and spat tobacco.

"Shouldn't say such about Mommy," he said. "What's that you got there?"

"Bobby's leg."

"Never was no count."

Mercer dropped it, splashing mud on his pants. Wind pelted rain against their backs, and dark sky moved over the ridge.

"Hill ain't going to hold," Mercer said.

"That trailer washes down in the road," Aaron said, "I'll just leave it lay and plow a new road around it. I ain't living nowhere else but Crosscut Ridge." He sighed and looked at the sky. Water ran from his eyebrows. "Sure did get late early today."

Mercer walked to the pickup where Coe sat and smoked. In the cab, Mercer held his wet shirt away from his body. He was suddenly cold. Coe dropped his cigarette out the window. Mercer dug in his pocket.

"Here's your knife," he said.

Coe took the knife and bounced it in his palm. He glanced at Mercer, then offered the knife.

"You might need it," Coe said.

"I can't take a man's knife."

"It's yours." Coe tossed it in Mercer's lap. "Ain't that good a knife anyway."

"Reckon he'll live?" Mercer said.

"If he don't, my name'll come up. I got to get off this hill."

Coe lit another cigarette and started the truck. He turned on the wipers and lights, and after a few seconds, curls of steam rose from the warming hood. The steady hum of rain enclosed the truck.

THE LEAVING ONE

The boy crouched at the end of the wooded ridge, smashing walnuts with a brick and using a nail to pry the nutmeat. Quartered green shells lay scattered around him. To knock more nuts from the tree, Vaughn needed a special rock, since the veer of flat ones was hard to control, and small stones would not dislodge the September walnuts clinging tightly to the limbs. If he waited until they fell on their own, squirrels would get the best. Vaughn found a plum-sized rock and sighted into the leaves, arm tensed to throw. He spun instead, staring wildly into the dense tree line that bordered the ridge.

Something was there. Something was in the woods.

He was too far from the house for it to be his mother and there were no near neighbors. The path behind him was empty. Vaughn scanned the brush for animal sign, seeing only dark silent woods capped by a narrow strip of sky between the hills. Vaughn shrugged. As his mother would say, a goose walked over his grave was all. He found his target clump of walnuts, missed his throw, and felt something in the woods again, closer now.

He moved into the shadow of trees and abruptly knew that a deer would be standing beyond the pine thicket ahead. His palms tingled and his fingers began to spread. As he neared the syrupy dark of the low pines, the feeling increased. Dropped needles, soft and brown, hushed his feet. Sap smell filled him. He circled the thicket and peered into a small empty clearing. The deer was gone, and with it, the strange pull of the woods. He stepped into the clearing and a man stood beside an oak as if shed from the tree.

He was an old man with long hair matted by leaf and twig. A deer-hide shirt draped loose over his body as though he had once been a bigger man. Ragged fringe tied oak leaves to his shirt.

The man raised his brown palm to show the rock. He tossed it underhand and when Vaughn caught it, the man was gone. Vaughn stared from the rock to the silent woods and felt scared, but he was twelve and knew he could outrun a man that old. He pitched the rock at the tree. The man stepped from behind the oak, holding the stone he'd caught. His face was lined like ironwood.

"Who are you?" Vaughn said.

"Depends on who you be."

"Vaughn."

"Who's your maw's people?"

"Boatman."

Dark holes speckled the old man's brief grin. "You look a Boatman," he said. "Got them slitty eyes all us got."

"Are we kin?"

"Elijah Boatman," the man said. "Lije they called me when they did. I'm your grandpaw."

"No you ain't. He's dead."

The man's narrow shoulders drooped as he limped across the clearing. "Your maw tell you that?"

Vaughn nodded. The man blew a burst of warm air against Vaughn's face.

"Feel that?" the man said.

"Yup."

"Still yet on my hind legs, ain't I. Do I look dead to you?"

"Well," Vaughn said. "You're kindly old."

Lije laughed, a low sound rising to a bellow that ended with a prolonged cough. He used Vaughn's shoulder to steady himself. His breath was raspy. His body bowed inside the stiff buckskin, and it seemed to Vaughn that only the man's clothes were holding him up. The woods were very quiet.

"How come you're dressed like that?" Vaughn said.

"It's the Boatman way," Lije said. "How come you ain't?"

Vaughn frowned and looked at the ground. He wore the same clothes as all the other boys on Redbird Ridge, ordered from Sears a size too large. His mother ironed

patches at the knees that stiffened his pants like stove-
pipes. Lije cleared his throat.

"A-using this rock to fetch out walnuts, are you?"

"Was."

"Rock's not much count for naught but finding
rock," Lije said. "Don't never aim a throw."

He stepped into the late afternoon sunlight cutting
over the western ridge. Vaughn followed until the man
suddenly turned to face him, holding a walnut. He closed
his eyes and cocked an arm, fringe drifting like a wing.
He threw the walnut over his shoulder. It arched high,
dropping through the boughs of yellow leaves. Several walnuts fell to earth.

The old man opened his eyes. "Leave one," he said.

The nuts lay beneath the tree in a diamond shape
with a large walnut in the center. Vaughn gathered them
quickly, winding them into the bottom of his shirt when
his pockets became too tight. He left the biggest and hurried to the man, who leaned on a maple by the game path.
Vaughn was aware of the wind's sliding chill and the old
man's withered body in his deer-hide shirt. He seemed
weaker now.

"Where was it?" Lije said. "The leaving one."

"In the middle."

The man nodded, grunting a long rumble from deep
within his chest. Wind moaned back and the two sounds
braided through the woods. Fading sunlight cooled the air.

"Be dark in a minute," Vaughn said.

"Will."

"Let's go to the house."

"Your maw'll not put me up. Don't say you seen me,
either. Swear by the dirt."

Vaughn nodded. Lije steaded himself and looked into the woods. "Never could abide no roof."

"Ours ain't the best," Vaughn said. "Leaks come spring."

Lije pointed at Venus faint above the distant ridge. "Only roof-hole I ever did crave."

"Evening star ain't a hole."

"Then how's that light get through?"

Vaughn tipped his head to the dim night sky. When he looked at Lije, the old man was moving into the woods, his knife sheath flapping deer-tail white. Hillside darkness took him swift as shadow. Vaughn looked at Venus again, remembering from school that it wasn't a star but a planet like earth, only closer to the sun. He walked slowly home, wondering who the old man was. Vaughn knew everyone who lived on the ridge and in the flanking hollows below the hill. Grandfathers whittled a lot and taught their grandsons how to fish. Lije was just old.

Vaughn dumped the walnuts on the pine slat porch of his mother's house. He scraped dirt from his boots on the top step and opened the door. A small dark bird veered past his shoulder and into the house, flying tight loops in the living room.

"Don't shut the door!" his mother said. "Open a window up."

She hurried to the kitchen, returning with a broom slanted across her body, bristles aimed high. "Where's it at?"

"Flew back out."

"Oh sweet Lord," she said. "A bird in the house is worst of all. Did it touch you?"

"No."

"Just a warning then. My opinion it's on your great-aunt down to Rocksalt. Her lungs don't work right in fall. I'll pray for her tonight."

She gathered a deep breath, went to the kitchen, and came out with salt mounded in her palm.

"Take a smidgeon, Vaughn," she said, "and throw it over your shoulder."

Martha pinched a finger's worth and timed her toss to match his. She threw more salt through the open doorway, then quickly yanked the door shut. Kneeling, she pressed her hands together and trickled a line of salt across the threshold. "Yea though I walk through the valley of the shadow of death, I shall fear no evil . . ."

Wind rattled the stovepipe, startling Martha. She stood and faced her son.

"I'm hungry," Vaughn said.

She smiled, relaxing. "Count on you to think of your belly."

They ate supper in the narrow kitchen. Above the metal-edged Formica table hung a portrait of Jesus, the only picture in the house. A breeze seeped beneath the window.

"You cold?" she said.

"No."

"How was school?"

Vaughn shrugged.

"What'd you learn?"

"Teacher said history ain't a straight line of time."

"What is it then?"

"Said history lays over itself like corn in a crib and we're all a cob." Vaughn shrugged and looked at the greasy plate. He began to lie. "Then he told about his family and asked about ours."

Martha stiffened, chin creeping up. "Your father was a good man," she said. "God sent him up to Ohio for work. Be back any season."

"Is my grandpaw really dead?"

Martha was silent for a long time and Vaughn knew she was turning Bible pages in her mind, searching an answer.

"He's dead to God," she said. "That makes him dead to me."

"But is he really?"

"No," she whispered.

"Is he old?"

"Eighty some."

"Where's he live?"

Martha looked away from the blue eyes of Jesus on the wall. She trailed a spoon across her plate. "Your grandpaw lives where the state puts people . . ." She stared at the devil's horns she'd made from gravy and shut her eyes. "It's a place for people who can't live by their ownself."

"How'd he get there?"

She used her spoon to close the curving horns etched into the gravy. She drew a fish and stared at the faded picture of Jesus. Her words rushed, rising and falling in a lilt.

"Lije run off to World War One and was a chaplain. He came home changed, and took to living on the other side of Shawnee Rock. Not no regular house, just out in the hills. He came down sometimes to see Mommy and us kids. Then the next war came and all my brothers got killed, three of the best boys you ever did see.

"Well, me and Sister and Mommy got took in by a neighbor woman to help raise us up. Her husband was a preacher, could make a possum take to gospel. He'd get everybody riled and head for the creek bank. When he was finished, that creek'd be half dry. And let me tell you, he'd hold a body under till they was nigh drowned. He was bear-stout, he was. People were right proud to claim they'd got saved by him.

"One spring, he done Sister that way and she passed out cold. Preacher lifted her out of the water limp as dead. That's when Lije ran out of the woods screaming like a bobcat. He'd been hid and watching everything. He took hold of Sister's shoulders and had a tug-of-war until the preacher let go. Lije laid her down and hunkered there beside her. Then he started kissing her mouth and rubbing her bubs. That's what people always did say, but what it was, he was drawing that creek water right out of her body. He spit it out and breathed into her mouth three times. He had a little bag tied to his waist, and he took and rubbed stuff on her neck and chest. Well, her breathing got regular. Her eyes opened up.

"Preacher lifted his King James and said Lije Boatman wasn't fit to live with decent folks. Said he was a devil. Said everybody seen how he'd done devil-stuff to his own daughter.

"Lije laughed. He looked at everybody and said, 'They ain't no devil. Only bad men.' He jumped the creek and ran up the hillside. The preacher claimed how Lije denying it just proved how evil he was. Said if they ain't no devil, they ain't no God, and if they ain't no God, then what were all these people lined up at the creek for.

"One by one, everybody walked into the creek. Only me and Sister stayed on the bank. The preacher yelled about getting sin cleaned plumb off him, and how the only way was letting the Lord see you like you was brung into the world. Preacher took his shirt off. He told his wife to undo her dress and she did. They was standing there in the water half naked. He went and took his britches down and everybody started taking their clothes off. It was a race to see who could show the Lord their true self first. The preacher laid in preaching and he went on till the lightning bugs had come and gone.

"Lije never visited no more but stayed in the woods some forty years. Then VISTA heard of him and brought him out of the hills. I heard he fought, but was weakly, sick with something. A man from the state went to the preacher's daughter and asked did she know who Lije's kin was. Next day she came out here packing food to give me. Said did I want to take Lije in. But I never. I sent my own daddy off like stock to a pen. I broke a commandment."

Martha's voice had faded to a hoarse whisper. She carried her plate to the sink, where she began washing it over and over, reciting the Lord's Prayer.

Vaughn left the table and slipped to his room and into bed. From outside came a barred owl's rising call. Moonlight soaked the yard and lit the woods beyond the house. Vaughn stared through the window, and though the sound grew louder, he could not see the owl. He lay listening to the bird, no longer able to hear his mother's droning voice.

After school the next day he heard the owl again and followed the sound to a tall oak. Lije sat beneath the tree. He blew into his cupped hands, making the eight tones that ended in a low gurgle. An answering call echoed from the dusky woods. Lije showed Vaughn how to duplicate the sound, and the owl answered once, then quit.

"Owl's just being civil until he knows you better," Lije said.

"When will he?"

"That's on you. People don't like owls because they live in graveyards, but an owl needs a big tree and grave-yard trees don't get cut down. Never be afraid on account of where something lives. That goes for people, too."

Vaughn decided not to tell him what his mother had said. Lije didn't act like a devil or look like one. He was more old than anything else, and Vaughn was glad to have a grandpaw, even if he wasn't quite right in the head. Vaughn knew that happened to old people. His fifth-grade teacher had broken her hip and when she returned to school, she wore different wigs each day and put lipstick on her nose. Vaughn thought that was worse than talking to owls.

On Saturday Vaughn sat in the white glare of a low noon sun and watched the woods. Softwood leaves, crisp with equinox color, floated them treetops near the sun. His pocket held leftover breakfast pork in case Lije was hungry. Vaughn sweated in the heat but stayed on the porch. Lije had said to wait, that a Boatman knew sign and if Vaughn wasn't anything else, he was a damn-sure Boatman. "Looking won't find nary a thing," Lije had said. "Just you set on lookout. It'll find you."

His mother's mumbling voice drifted from the house, talking to Jesus. Vaughn had tried it once when his mother was in the garden. He sat in her chair facing the

picture in its plastic filigreed frame. Jesus didn't answer.
Vaughn talked some more but Jesus never said a word and
soon Vaughn felt stupid, hearing his voice in the kitchen
with no one there. At the bottom of the picture was a
company name and the words SCRANTON, PENNSYLVANIA.
Vaughn figured that was where Jesus lived, and on a school
map he'd seen that Scranton wasn't too far from Bethlehem. He talked to his teacher, who said there was more
than one Bethlehem, there might be five or six, maybe a
dozen. Jesus didn't have a real home, he lived everywhere.

Behind Vaughn the screen door rubbed on hinge
straps cut from an old tire. His mother crossed the porch
and stroked the back of his head.

"What all I said the other night don't have much to
do with you," she said. "That's old and done. You're a
good boy, Vaughn. You'll make a man one day."

"I'm hungry," he said.

"Then you're among the living." She sighed and
looked into the woods. "You stay close by the house
today."

"How come?"

"Just feel it's all. There's a prayer meeting tonight
and I want you to go with me. You hear?"

Vaughn nodded, staring at the ground as his mother
went in the house. She didn't attend church often, had
never forced him to join. Maybe tonight Lije would go,
too. They'd sit together and everyone would know Lije
was his grandfather.

The sudden absence of sound lifted Vaughn's head
to the empty sky. He peered into dark brush between the
trees. A red-tailed hawk lofted from a gum tree and glided

through the open limbs of the ridge. Vaughn crossed the yard and entered the woods. Autumn was all around him.

The dry rustle of leaves drew Vaughn up the steep ridge slope and down the hill. He stopped at a creek twisting through cudweed in the dark hollow. A frog splashed into the creek. Vaughn turned, and another frog leaped from the bank. The shifting tendrils of a willow swayed apart, releasing sun shafts from its shade. Vaughn moved to the light, stepped through the willow's overhang, and stood below an outcrop of shale. Clear water gushed through a gap in the rock. Above it, Lije was sitting cross-legged in the sun, his face strained and lichen gray. Vaughn climbed the slippery cliff and squatted beside him.

"You're good," Lije said. "Come straight here without no maundering about. Didn't tucker me too bad, a-towing you."

His eyes were filmy and his voice came faint. A vine held his long hair back. Vaughn breathed through his mouth to avoid the smell. Lije grinned.

"Fox piss," he said. "Cuts man-stink awful good. Slept in an old den last night. Got you something, too."

He opened a belt pouch and withdrew a shiny piece of quartz.

"Shooting star," he said. "Seen it fall last night. Points all busted off when it hit. Ever saw one?"

"Yup."

"You take and hold this up tonight and see if it don't match them others. A fell star ain't easy to get."

Vaughn had learned in school that stars were gas balls a billion miles away. Quartz lay thick in the hills and it glittered in the sandstone creek beds. Vaughn wondered just how crazy his grandfather was.

"I brought some breakfast," Vaughn said.

"Done ate berries and such. Went dryland fishing but the frost beat me out."

"You really my grandpaw?"

"Found me, didn't you."

"Maw said you were in some kind of state place."

"I let them keep me till the time came."

"She said people think you're a devil."

"You go by that?"

Vaughn slowly shook his head. He wasn't certain what he believed but knew that sitting here was right. Lije stood, leaning on Vaughn. He coughed and spat, and continued to cough a thick, wet sludge. He stepped to the cliff edge and jumped. A sapling eased him to the earth. Vaughn slid sideways down the loose rock face and followed the limping man into the woods.

"We going fishing?" Vaughn said.

"No."

"Where we headed for?"

"The where ain't much count against the how. We're not just traipsing these hills, boy. We're walking with the woods."

Vaughn remembered his mother's warning to stay near the house. If he was going back, now was the time. He'd come to the creek often but had never crossed it, and could get home easily from here. The woods didn't scare Vaughn except at night, when his mother said spirits roved.

Vaughn followed Lije deeper into the woods. No matter who the man was, he was still a grown-up and Vaughn knew he'd be safe. Lije plucked a long, dusky feather from the brush. "This way," he said, and moved east. A hundred yards away, he found a second feather. Lije glided through the woods, dipping a shoulder and bending a knee to avoid low limbs, moving like a shadow. Vaughn plodded behind, his face marked by thorn and branch.

Their route shifted with each new feather as they traveled beyond the logged-out land and into older woods near Shawnee Rock. Giant trees crowded together, casting dark shade. Lije headed east, away from the afternoon sun slicing the woods. The man wasn't talking and Vaughn had never been this far from home. If he turned back, he'd be lost.

An hour later, Lije lifted an arm and tipped his fingers. Vaughn moved to him, smelling the buckskin musk and odor of fox. The woods air chilled.

"Feathers done," Lije whispered. "Deer now."

Where, Vaughn thought.

Lije aimed his chin at the ridgeline. "Other side yonder." He squatted. "Sign," Lije muttered. "Spy it."

Vaughn mentally divided the earth into lanes and searched each row carefully. Weeds pushed through rotting leaves. A cicada shell lay beside pale nut shavings left by a squirrel.

"Don't look for nothing," Lije said. "The nose and ears is first cousin to the eyes."

Vaughn closed his eyes and imagined a deer weaving along the hollow and up the ridge. It moved slowly, chewing shrub, alert to sound. The buck looked directly at Vaughn with black eyes, very old. It held the stare a long time, then turned away.

Vaughn opened his eyes. In the forest floor before him lay a narrow path of bent grass and dead leaves turned damp-side up. He stared hard and the trail faded, becoming the bottom of the woods.

"I saw it," Vaughn said.

"Boatman can't help but to."

"It's gone now."

"Because you're looking again."

Lije limped up the slope, bent from the waist, following sign. He coughed steadily. Vaughn closed his eyes and the deer appeared before him. When he opened them, Lije's buckskinned body moved along the trail. They eased down a steep bank to the soft ground of a rain gully. Lije followed the creek twenty yards before moving upslope to the next fold of land. The setting sun was on their backs.

In a basin laced with squawroot, Lije stood erect. He turned in a slow circle, eyes closed and arms extended, his fingertips quivering in the silent woods. His mouth hung slack. A deep breath forced his wet cough.

"He's pranking with me," Lije said. "Doubled on us or hid, one."

"Could be anywhere."

"But he ain't." Lije's whisper was weak. "There's only one place he's at and that's wherever he is." His fingers squeezed Vaughn. "Where'd he go, Boatman?"

"Over that ridge." Vaughn pointed without thought.

"How do you know?"

"Don't."

"But you know."

Vaughn nodded.

"What else?" Lije said.

"Something's behind us."

"What?"

"Can't rightly say."

"You feared?"

"No."

"It's your shadow's shadow then."

Lije coughed and began limping up the ridge. Vaughn looked into the dark silence of the woods and realized that night was an hour away and his mother would be mad. She'd spend all evening telling the picture of Jesus what an evil boy she had. When he came home, she'd make him kneel on stones.

Vaughn climbed the hill and stood beside Lije. The fading sunshine flung their shadows over the land. Lije's outline flowed across the earth, disappearing between two huge and ancient oaks. They were seven feet apart, too close for trees their size. Vaughn's shadow ended halfway to the oaks.

"There it is," Lije said.

"The deer?"

"No. Deer's one led us here. Him and the hawk. That there's the go-over place."

The twin oaks rose like massive legs, their branches twining overhead, blocking sky. Between the trees lay a sunken strip of earth. The arching stems of Solomon's-seal formed a boundary to the dark space beneath the oaks. Lije walked down the hill into his shadow. Beyond the steep surrounding hillsides were the crests of further hills that melted into the dusk. Crickets began their sunset creaking. Lije was halfway down the hill when Vaughn saw movement to his left.

A huge deer emerged from the brush with a sixteen-point rack spreading from a tapered head. He had never seen a deer that big. Hunters killed them before they got that old. The buck stood calm and still, watching Vaughn. Its dark eyes were deep as time.

"Grandpaw," Vaughn whispered.

Wind closed leaves around the retreating buck. Vaughn ran down the hill to Lije, who stood before the giant oaks. The noise of the deer circled the trees.

"I saw it," Vaughn said. "I saw the deer."

"No," said Lije. "He showed himself."

Lije entered the space between the trees. Branches rattled overhead and whippoorwills began their call. Lije sat cross-legged in the center of the trees, smearing gray ash over his face. From inside his shirt, he pulled an oval stone threaded on a thong around his neck. He lifted it over his head and offered it to his grandson. Vaughn stepped between the trees and pressed his hand over the rock.

"This'll be yours now," Lije said. "My pa-paw give me it."

"What is it?"

"He never said."

Lije's body began to rock. He leaned his face close to Vaughn and gripped him by his arms. His eyes glittered fierce.

"Sing you the be I song," Lije said. "Sing you what land made me. The oak shadow is be I. Dream tinker is my drum. The eyes in the woods you feel alone. Wind-breath from a cave. Deerprint, birdcall, bobcat keen. The leaf be I. The leaf be I. The leaf be I."

Acorns rained to the ground while screeching squirrels raced from limb to limb. Lije's face was paling fast.

A yellow butterfly circled a blur around his head. He slowly tilted backwards into swirling leaves and settled to the earth, pulling Vaughn with him, onto his body. They held the stone together, pressed tight between their palms.

"Leave me lay here after," Lije said. "You be the Boatman now."

The roots of both oaks interlocked below; their branches welded overhead. The red-tailed hawk rustled to a landing on the oak's low crotch. The sounds of night swarmed the woods. A bobcat's high-pitched scream pierced the quickening wind. Leaves whirled the air. From far away came the rumbling bellow of a bear. The wind and animal sound increased until it seemed to Vaughn that all the hills were rushing to the oaks. He shut his eyes and pushed his face against his grandfather's silent chest.

Wind moved away and the autumn woods slowly hushed. Vaughn lay a long time before pushing himself up. Lije was still, his sightless eyes staring into the tree limbs overhead. Vaughn's imprint lay on his body outlined by red oak leaves. The stone was in Vaughn's hand, and though he thought he should feel scared, he wasn't. Beside him stood the ancient buck.

The deer pawed a bare place next to Lije and urinated against the earth. It moved to Lije's other side and repeated itself, marking its own, and hobbled into the woods on a weak back leg.

Vaughn strung the oval stone over his neck. He took the feathers and stepped from the cold alley between the oaks. An owl called and another answered until their sound filled the woods. Vaughn chose the biggest feather and shaped its tines, drawing them tight to the tip, and stretched his arm between the oaks. The leaving feather settled to the buckskin husk of Lije. Vaughn began walking toward the red glow of sun behind the western hill.

Dusk pushed over the ridge and across the land. Vaughn went down the slope and up a dark hollow to the hill where Lije had found the last feather. Vaughn stopped, unable to remember the direction they had come. He faced the oaks beyond the ridge and held the stone between his hands. Behind him something big came up the hill. He thought it was the deer but heard no swish of leaf or crackling twig. Vaughn pressed the stone to his chest. He felt the force move slowly to his back and stop. Overhead, full dark arrived. Silence flowed through the woods.

The thing was suddenly gone, and Vaughn knew what it was, and why he was not afraid. The hill had come up the hill. The hill would lead him home. He turned and walked into the night, avoiding branches easily. In his hand the stone began to warm.

HORSEWEED

William plucked beads of hardened plaster from his trowel and wiped them on the bucket's edge. The wall joints had to be smooth as snow. This job might lead to another and the Brants wanted everything perfect. The Brants owned the sheetrock, the plaster, and the red rug under the drop cloth. Until the job was finished, they owned William eight hours a day. Only the ability belonged to William; he'd had to rent the tools.

Mrs. Miriam Brant walked into the room to check his progress, wearing a loose housecoat with nothing underneath. William looked away from her thighs and dipped the trowel. His wife's legs weren't as good but they were more familiar. Miriam tapped a red fingernail against the wall.

"I want your opinion on a room in back," she said.

He followed her through a long hall to the bedroom. A three-panel mirror filled a corner, and small rugs lay on the carpet. She bent from the waist, pointing to a web of ripples that puckered the wallpaper like a burn scar. The housecoat fell open to her navel.

"Work in here," she said, "is never good enough to suit me."

William looked past her face to the store-bought blanket on the bed, feeling bad for her. She was from Bobcat Hollow but had married a lawyer and moved to town. Her husband refused to let her family visit except during election years. William's fingers brushed the dimpled wall. The room was quiet and big, and he could hear his own breathing. He wondered when her husband got off work.

"Too much water in the glue," he said.

"Always something."

"Man ought not to leave a job that way."

"Maybe you could do better."

William looked at her legs, thinking of his wife at home all day. He lifted his head and spoke quietly.

"My daddy knew your daddy."

Miriam hugged her housecoat together and sat on the bed, shoulders slumped, head down.

"I couldn't wait to get out of that holler," she said. "Now I'm just as stuck here as I was there. You still live on the ridge?"

"Guess I'm stuck there, too."

William returned to the living room, where he skimmed plaster over the seam and feathered the edges. The work was nearly complete; tomorrow he would sand. At an outside faucet he cleaned the tools, watching the steady stream of water sparkle in the sun. Miriam waved from the window. William stared at her a long time before getting into his truck. He hoped he wouldn't regret his decision to leave. He'd always liked her when they were kids.

William slowly drove the blacktop home, glad to be out of Rocksalt. He passed a new video dish perched among felled trees and wondered what his father would have thought of such a thing. Two years ago he'd told his father about a job with a construction crew in town.

"A man's lucky to have these hills," his father had said.

"I know it," William said. "But they ain't exactly ours no more."

"Town never was either."

William's father spat dark phlegm against the clay dirt yard. Coal dust filled his pores, blending his face into the night. His voice took on the timbre of a father speaking to a son, not to a man he trusted underground, working an illegal mine.

"Don't you do like your grandpaw done."

William stared at his boots. Years back, during the first mine strikes, his grandfather had made whiskey to keep his kids in clothes. A government man shotgunned him as he unloaded forty quarts of liquor at Blue Lick River. His body fell into the muddy water and the family buried an empty coffin.

"I'm not Grandpaw," William had said. "And you're not me."

Tools rattled in the truck bed as William drove up the hill and out Crosscut Ridge to his house. Three dogs chased through the dust, jumping at the pickup. William squatted, pushing his fingers in the fur behind each dog's ears. He found several ticks, their bodies stretched tight like kernels of white corn. He twisted one free and squeezed it between thumb and finger. The tick burst in a spray of dark blood.

The heavy scent of venison stew drifted from the house, and William wondered how many meals were left on the doe. His daughters needed more meat. Inside, his wife, Connie, held the baby on her hip. Sarah sat on the floor, banging a spoon against a pot. Ruth rushed to her father.

"How many'd you get?" she said.

"Eight," William said. "Three off Blackie. Two off Hubcap. So how many ticks off Duke?"

She grunted over stubby fingers. Connie turned and pushed stray hair behind an ear. Afternoon sun washed her skin, softening the shadows below her eyes.

"How's town?" she said.

"About done."

"Take your clothes off before you set down."

"I'll take them off," he said, thinking of Miriam.

Five kinds of paneling formed the bedroom's tight walls. His favorite depicted a scene of three grouse flying over tall grass. He scanned as if hunting and decided it would take a twenty-gauge with a cylinder bore. From the right position, a man could bring down all three birds. He studied a mirror with taped cracks. White plaster powder coated his face, and he resembled his father except for the color of the dust. William thought of the bathroom Connie wanted. Either that or a trailer, she had said. William was afraid she'd rather move to town.

In the living room, he sat on the end of the couch. Clear plastic covered the other half. As they paid if off, Connie exposed the vinyl in small increments, slicing the plastic with a kitchen knife. William understood that this was a display of her thrift—she deserved indoor plumbing. Town water was nine miles away and moving closer every day. He waved to the crew each morning on his way to Rocksalt, envious of their steady work. To add a bathroom, he needed three times the money from last year's tobacco crop, but the auction brought less every fall.

Connie called him to eat and he walked to the table, watching his daughters rinse their hands in an old lard bucket. Roofing tar plugged a hole in the bottom. The girls laughed around the pail hauled from the well at the end of the ridge. Splashed water clung to their blond hair.

After supper, William slipped into his hunting jacket that smelled of earth and game. He pulled a rifle from the closet and checked the breech. Walnut whorls patterned the stock in light and dark. It had belonged to his father, and his grandfather. William often wondered who he'd give it to. He dropped some bullets in a pocket.

"Going out the ridge," he said.

"If I didn't know better," Connie said, "I'd think you had a woman out there."

"What I got is better." He forced a grin. "Back by dark."

"Watch for snakes. They're bad this year."

The dogs followed him as he climbed the hill, gauging fallen trees for winter firewood. Overlapping shadows flowed across the forest floor. When he neared a hickory, the hounds began to whine, their dark eyes showing fear. He loaded the rifle and the dogs ran yelping back to the house. He recalled his grandfather's voice, telling William moonshine stories as a boy.

"You take your dogs to a tree where you don't want them to follow you no more," the old man had said. "Let each dog smell of the gun. Then you kill one. The rest ain't much count for hunting after that, but they'll not lead the law to a still. I done it many a time."

William stepped around the hickory to stand above his dog's small grave. King had been old and slow, nearly blind, his favorite. He nodded to the humped earth and walked deeper into the woods. The land crested to a plateau of three hills where two ridges tapered down to the creek. He headed east, away from people, and eased down the hill to a lower ridge. He followed it to a limestone cliff and circled the rocks to a narrow hollow. At its end, he climbed onto a low knob ringed by hills. He listened carefully in each direction. A mourning dove moaned and high leaves brushed on a breeze. He hunched over, eyes intent on the ground. He saw a boot print and tensed his hands on the rifle.

The track was his own from before.

William topped the knob and grinned. Planted on ten-inch centers stood fifty-one hemp plants gently rocking in the breeze. William had never smoked hemp. It simply grew, the same as corn his grandfather had used for mash. Like ginseng and tobacco, hemp had become a valuable weed. Town people would buy a load and he'd sell it cheap. All he wanted were bathroom fixtures, two hundred feet of PVC pipe, and a mirror for Connie.

He walked through his garden, breaking off weak branches and pulling new shoots. He turned the leaves to check for worms. After pruning he leaned against a sycamore and listened to a whippoorwill wail into the surrounding hardwood hills. William knew hemp was safer than moonshine because the knob belonged to the mine company. A new law allowed the state to steal family land with hemp on it, but the government had always left big coal operators alone. Most of the companies came from out of state, and except for bribes in Frankfort, the money went out of state, too. William's father had said that was the reason Kentucky had such weak reclamation laws.

Of five miners working illegally during the oil embargo, three went to prison, one got rich, and thirty tons of earth fell on William's father. Everyone on the hill helped dig him out. After the funeral William worked town construction for three months. Instead of drinking with the other men after work, he saved his money and bought his own tools. When the job ended he was laid off while everyone else moved to another site. The foreman said that he didn't mix well. William sold his tools for half of what he'd paid and began searching the hills for wild hemp to transplant on the hidden knob.

Saw briers rattled over the hill. William twitched his head, aiming his ears in that direction. The steady sound was loud enough for large game. He climbed down the back of the knob and circled the downwind side, placing each foot carefully to avoid the noise of leaf or fallen limb. Only a fawn would wander into briers. Its mother would be near. William flicked off the rifle's safety.

At the edge of the woods, he knelt behind an oak and sniffed sassafras blending with pine sap. The whippoorwill's cry was very loud, a warning. William leaned his head and rifle around the tree. His vision skipped along the ridge to the base of the knob and slowly up the steep bank. Sweat trickled down his sides. A man stood thirty yards away at the lip of the knob. Hemp plants swayed above his head.

William peered through the scope of his grandfather's gun. He lowered the rifle past the man's face to the center of his chest and leaned against the tree to steady his aim, knowing the hills would swallow the sound. He inhaled, and let the air out slow and careful.

The man turned in a small circle, gazing around the hills. William breathed normally again. He would not rush a killing shot. The man limped to a sapling and climbed over the knob, panting like a chased fox. With trembling hands he pulled his pants leg to the knee. William moved the scope to the man's bare calf. In the center of a dark swelling were two red puncture marks.

William pivoted around the oak and locked the safety behind the trigger. In three days, he could pretend to find the man and drag him out of the woods. The man would never remember the hemp. He'd lose his leg and not return.

The sun began its final slide behind the far hill when William stood, propped his rifle over his shoulder, and stepped into the deep shade of the woods. Connie expected him home by now. Their daughters would be in bed and he and Connie would lie on the couch and make silent love so as not to wake them. William glanced at the dimming sky and wished he hadn't seen the snake-bit leg. Now he couldn't shoot the man, and worse, he couldn't just walk away.

William moved down the bank and climbed the knob, forcing himself not to look at the hemp. The man was small and wiry and William was surprised that he was so young. His eyes were wide as bottle caps.

"Copperhead got me," said the man.

"Big or little?"

"Big."

"You're lucky. Babies are the worst."

"Lucky," said the man.

William opened his pocketknife and sliced the man's pants along the seam.

"Got a lighter?" William said.

The man slid a sweaty hand into his pocket and handed William a blue book of matches. On its cover the coal company's name was embossed in gold.

"I just work for them," the man said. "I don't own it."

"Shut up."

William lit a match and passed the knife blade through the flame. The shiny metal blackened. He straddled the man's thigh and made a short, deep slit in his calf. He lifted the knife and turned his wrist to cut again. The two lines crossed at one of the holes left by the snake. William pressed his mouth to the wound. Sucked air squeaked, and liquid filled his mouth. He turned his head to spit and repeated the process on the other hole. William cut a patch from the man's shirttail and covered the wound, tying it with strips of cloth. The man lay on his back, cheek against the dirt. Vomit pooled beside his face.

William spat until his mouth was dry, then ran his tongue along his gums to check for sores. He knew he'd swallowed some but that didn't matter; stomach acid was stronger than venom. The man rustled dead leaves, struggling to sit.

"What'd they send you for?" William said. "They done mined this land out."

"Just running tests."

"Up here?"

"No. When the snake hit me, I came this way. Figured I'd build a fire and somebody'd see it."

"You'd do that, wouldn't you. You'd burn the woods down."

"Nothing here but some kind of horseweed."

The moon rose above the hemp as if towed by the setting sun. The man's clothes were ripped from briars. A gold band glinted on his left hand, and William wondered if he had kids.

"Live in town?" William said.

"All my life," the man said. "We'd like to move out, but I don't know."

"It ain't easy around here."

"Neither is town. Prices are high as a cat's back."

William reached for his rifle and stood. The man stopped talking, eyes growing wide again. He leaned back, breathing hard. William emptied the rifle of bullets, pulled the man to his feet, and handed him the gun.

"Use this to walk with," William said. "You parked on the fire road?"

The man nodded.

"Try not to bang the scope."

He led the man across the knob and down the back slope into the woods. Tree frogs ceased their noise. Night came over the eastern hills, passed the men, and seeped along the ridge. Starlight spread through open sky. At the foot of the hill, William squatted to drink from the creek. He waited for the man to thrash through heavy growth along the bank.

"Think I ought to wash my leg?" the man said.

"This water might not be the cleanest on account of the mines."

"Then why are you drinking it?"

"All we got," William said. "Ever notice how town water always tastes like pipe?"

"Never did," said the man. "What's your name?"

William stood quickly. "Got a mile to go, uphill."

He began following the creek past tree roots slithering down the bank. A bobwhite call floated through the trees. William remembered that his father and grandfather had walked this creek home from the mines, and he was suddenly glad he'd had no sons. The responsibility of land would end with him. Men's lives ran in bursts of work, drink, and quick death, while women wore down slow and steady, like a riverbank at a sharp curve. He'd urge his daughters to move, but they'd probably stay and give him grandsons. One day William would be old and telling a boy about helping a coal man who didn't deserve it. He wondered what the state would find to outlaw in his grandsons' time.

An hour later, William and the man reached the pickup parked on the one-lane fire road. The late-model truck had new tires, high shocks, and the coal company name on each door.

"I can make it from here," the man said.

"Nice truck."

"Only reason I took the damn job," the man said. "Free gas and a company truck. It runs better than I do." He patted the hood. "What do I owe you?"

William shook his head and looked away. He checked the rifle scope and wiped moisture from the barrel. The man climbed into the cab.

"That wasn't horseweed up there, was it?" the man said.

"I don't know," William said. "I don't raise horses."

"Far as I know," the man said, "you don't raise a thing."

He started the truck, drifting exhaust along the ridge. Headlights splayed through the trees as he backed along the narrow road. When the engine faded, the sounds of night began again.

William moved through darkness, following the creek. At the fork, he climbed the hill to Crosscut Ridge. He felt momentarily glad that his grandfather and father were dead and unable to know he'd helped the man live. His father would have left the man snake-bit, and his grandfather would have shot him. If William's own grandson understood his decision, he'd give the rifle to the boy.

He chuckled to himself, thirty-two years old and talking to an unborn child. After his grandfather died, he'd once heard his father late at night, telling the old man about the landing on the moon. His father swore that TV people had invented it for money. The proof, he whispered into the darkness, was that nobody ever went back.

Connie was asleep when William came home. He sat on the bed and spoke in her ear, promising a mirror with a built-in light for the bathroom. She wiggled naked across his lap. Moonlight gleamed through the window, outlining his hand along her hip. She unbuttoned his shirt and he remembered Miriam. He tightened his eyes to erase her from his mind. His father filled the gap. He stood tall and coal-dirty, holding a dinner bucket and helmet. Connie kissed William's neck and brushed her fingers along his back. He thought of Miriam again, and this time let her stay. His father had been smiling. The big seam he'd found would make the family rich.

OLD OF THE MOON

Cody told everyone within range how wicked he'd been for thirty years of his life. He carried a pistol. He drank a pint of whiskey every day. He once tied a man to a hickory tree with old barbed wire and stole his boots.

"I left him skunk-bait and barefooted," Cody would say. "I was straight flat bad back then, but not no more."

He'd clear his throat as if to spit, then quietly use a handkerchief and tell about a mare he'd won in an all-night card game. He was riding home at dawn when a summer storm dappled the road dust. The horse veered to shelter beneath a silver maple. Cody broke a switch and beat the mare's back legs until it stepped onto the muddy trail. Lightning shot from a thunderhead and struck the horse. The mare slowly toppled, its body black and stiff, pinning Cody to the road. When the storm passed he watched steam rise from the mare's hide.

The next day Cody shaved his beard, gave away his rifle, three pistols, two quarts of liquor, and nine decks of greasy cards. He quit cigarettes and coffee. He joined the Clay Creek Church of God. When the pastor died, Cody offered to fill in. Within a month, he'd doubled the small congregation by offering himself as proof of the Lord's work. "If a grade-A son of a bitch like me can get saved," he told people, "you can, too." Cody still had the same hard eyes, but where they used to be mean as a bear, now they looked like he could tame one.

In early spring, he carried a small red Bible east along a dirt road humped in the middle by weeds. Every mile, he nailed fliers to trees, advertising his first tent revival. The woods closed in, narrowing the road to a path that led to Tar Cutler's house. Tar was old as stone. He lived in a section of woods that people were afraid of, near Shawnee Rock, and was related to half the county. He'd fired shots at VISTA workers, census takers, and tax men. Tar hadn't been to church since the preachers had given up the Old Testament for the New, and Cody figured if he could save a sinner like Tar, all his kin would join the church.

At the top of the hill Cody walked among the shadowed hardwood trees. He had a flashlight but wanted to save the batteries for the night walk back. The air chilled, smelling of rain. Tar's house threw shade down the hill, blending with the darkness of the woods. Cody shouted but no one answered. He stomped the porch in case Tar was going deaf, yelled again, and opened the door. A terrible smell rushed out, the nauseating sweet stench of rotten meat. Cody didn't want to go inside, but felt he had to in case it was a dead dog that Tar hadn't buried yet. He covered his nose and stepped into an empty kitchen. Spiderwebs spanned the room corners. Tar was lying in his bed, eyes closed, a half-smile on his face. His shoulder and arm had been gnawed by rats.

Cody spat on the floor, angry at having come all this way for nothing. Without Tar's relatives, the revival would be a flop. The same people would come who always went to church: old people afraid of death, single women with kids, and men trying to please their wives. Cody suddenly grinned. He would tell everyone that just before Tar died, he'd been saved.

Cody dragged a chair beside the bed, surprised to find a tape recorder lying on the blanket. Tar had no phone, plumbing, or electricity, and he wouldn't own a tape recorder. Cody blew the dust away. Through the clear plastic window he could see a tape. Since Tar couldn't read or write, Cody thought the tape might be a will. Maybe old Tar had money buried somewhere he wouldn't mind donating to the church.

He carried the recorder to the porch, rewound the cassette, and pressed the play button. The tape recorder hissed. A man cleared his throat, whinnied a laugh, and said hello. Furniture scraped the floor. The voice began talking, shaky at first, then with more confidence. Cody held the tape recorder in his lap and listened to Tar Cutler speak.

———

I'm sitting in the bedroom of a house I built fifty-nine years ago. The only color to the hills is pine. We had one snow that mostly melted off, but there's some places the sun won't reach, shade strips running east, where snow lays like rope. You can hear sound a long ways off. The end of this ridge has always had my people living on it and I'm the last. My wife died and my kids left. I used to have a truck but I burnt the clutch out using it to plow my garden.

Worst thing I ever did was outlive my wife. Women live hard here. It ain't that men have it easy, I got a brother had a tree fall on him logging the woods, but women just don't get the off-time a man does. Anymore, there's not much left for me but waiting on winter, then waiting on spring. Time piles up like brush. You burn it in the fall and all you remember are the glowing cinders. I got ash heaps everywhere I look.

A road was built twenty-six years ago and instead of hauling things in, it took coal out. When the mines shut, my sons left to find work. Then my girls went off hunting husbands on account of all the boys gone. Now they want me to teach their kids the olden ways, who our family is, and how we lived. Thing is, I ain't aiming to leave. I visited my second daughter once, up in Ohio, and it didn't suit me long. She gave me a tape recorder and extra batteries. Said to send them tapes. Telling ain't hardly the same with no kids to listen at me, but here goes anyhow. I wasn't born yet, but many a winter night I've listened to my grandpaw tell this by the fire. He heard it off his daddy back before the Silver War.

My great-great-aunt Dorothy had a baby girl. Its name was Rose. Dorothy went up Flatgap Ridge, packing little Rose on her back, rigged in a baby board. Dorothy was a full-blood Shawnee Indian and that made Rose half. The spring sun was warm as biscuits. Only Judas tree was in blossom, white and pink, set low against the hardwoods. At the hilltop three ridges joined together, then split off and each followed its own creek. There's a wind up there, always was. If a man built a windmill to run a generator, he'd have light to burn all night.

Well, that wind blew Dorothy's smell through the woods, and that smell drew a bear. They sleep hard in the winter and wake up hungry, ready to eat an anvil. The bear tracked her a quarter-mile and Dorothy never heard it. Maybe she was singing loud, I don't know. It's as natural for a woman to sing to her baby as a bear to eat meat. You can't fault the hills for what happens in them. Some people blame God, but I don't think he is too bad off worried over what goes on here.

That bear, he came busting out of the woods quick as double triggers, running straight for Dorothy. Brush was flying behind it. Dorothy made a half-turn and its front paw swiped at her. She ducked. Its claws grazed her and tore out a little twist of hair. She took off running down the hill but the bear didn't follow.

At Lick Fork Creek, Dorothy untied the goat-hide harness, let the straps off her shoulders, and swung Rose around in front of her. I reckon Dorothy fainted. Next thing she was laying on the creek bank and claimed not to remember much after. Dogs at her sister's house raised a ruckus when she came up the holler. Her clothes were brier-tore. She was all over in blood, and her sister thought she fell off a cliff. She calmed Dorothy down and asked what was the matter and Dorothy opened her arms to show her baby. Rose's head was gone. The bear had tore the head clean off that baby.

Dorothy's sister had some hen in her, and she took charge right swift. Sent a kid for her husband, Wayne, who was planting taters way top a hillside. Now Wayne was a good man and a hard worker. They say he never had the sense God gave a goose, but I'd say his smart was different, that's all.

He come off the hill and his wife told him to ride and get his brother and then Dorothy's husband. Said go up the hillside and fetch that baby's head. It had to be buried with the baby or there'd be a spirit walking the ridge. Some people claim the new preachers drove the spirits off, but I'd say not. What got run off is the knowing about them. Spirits are like electric wires, they can run a heater or they can kill a man, and they ain't to be fooled with unless you got a gob of luck to risk.

Wayne tied a bag to his waist, took his pistol, and rode upcreek, reining the workhorse back and forth on firm ground. Lower Lick fed into Clay Creek, and Wayne's brother lived on the fork. Clabe was scrawny-legged with a big belly. He liked to eat and he liked to fish, and his whole life he wasn't more than three or four miles from that creek. Said he took a headache if he strayed too far.

Clabe and Wayne rode double with Clabe's dog following behind. They found Jim clearing land. He laughed at his brothers-in-law weighing the horse down, the sweat-foam sticking to their pants. Jim propped a double-bit ax across his shoulder and came down the slope. Clabe's muzzle-loader and Wayne's pistol took the smile square away from him.

"Dorothy," Jim said.

"She's all right," said Clabe.

They slid off the horse and rubbed the inside of the pants legs. The dog jumped on Clabe's boot, pink tongue hanging sideways. He pushed it down and moved away.

"It's the baby, then," Jim said.

"Up on Flatgap," said Clabe.

"Bad?"

"Don't get no worser."

"How?"

"Bear."

Jim swung at the dog, and sank the ax in the ground to the handle. The dog squalled across the clay dirt yard, spraying blood. Its yellow tail lay beside the buried ax head. Jim went in the house for his flintlock rifle and Wayne squatted beside the dog tail.

"Never did see one off a dog," he said.

"Get your eyes full," Clabe said.

"Might mean something."

"By God, you're getting bad off as an old cure-witch, trying to read a dog's hind end."

"Ought not to make fun," Wayne said. "Might come back on you."

Wayne spat between his legs, took off his belt, and ran it through the loops the opposite way. Clabe watched and didn't laugh. Used to, everybody went by sign and peculiar weather. I've carpentered that way myself. Fresh-cut green wood'll bow, cup, or warp all depending on where the moon's at. You take and build by the moon and your rafters will bend with the earth. I got that off my grandpaw and a keener man never hammered lumber. One time a board wouldn't fit and he told me to trim it, and I asked him how much to cut.

"A frog over," he said.

"What size frog?"

"Regular."

"Facing in or away?"

"Crossways."

"Stretched out or humped up?"

"It's ready to jump, boy. You're slow as Christmas."

He built three houses that way and they're still yet lived in, the standingest houses you ever did see. They'll outlast these hills.

Well, them boys set off for Flatgap Ridge. They left the horse at the house and took Clabe's dog and a bluetick Jim owned. The spring woods were greening slow, only the oaks holding back. Clabe whispered to Wayne.

"Don't tell Jim about the baby's head. We'll get it when he ain't looking close. You seen the way he done that dog."

"About like Peter, ain't he."

"What?" Clabe said. "Who?"

"When the man told Peter about Jesus getting caught, Peter cut his ear off."

"His own?"

"No. The man who said it."

"I ain't got time to argue the Book with you. Just don't let on to Jim, hear."

On top of the ridge, Jim found bear tracks and the place it ran out of the woods at. Leaves were kicked up and branches broke. He knelt in the path beside a patch of sticky red dirt. "My little girl," he said. "My baby Rose."

Clabe and Wayne looked in hollow logs, down a groundhog hole, and under berry thickets but couldn't find the head. Jim put both hands in the blood and rubbed it on his gun barrel. His voice came cruel. "Don't a one of you take a shot when we find that bear. It's mine to kill." He raised the rifle and tipped his head back, screaming a terrible sound. "Whistle up them dogs," he said. "And lay back from me."

To be much count, a hunting dog has got to be raised careful. One of my uncles treated dogs better than his own children, loving on his pups like a bird does eggs. When he was to hunt, these dogs ate better than family. His kids got scraps. Now this same uncle was a hard one in the woods. If a dog lost trail and circled back to him, my uncle didn't think nothing of killing that dog. He'd just shoot it and go on, leave it lay for the buzzards. His kids all growed up fine.

Jim's bluetick trailed the bear off the ridge, straight down the hill to a gully. Fresh prints held groundwater under a black willow. Wayne and Clabe were right smart back of Jim, and the late-day sun cut low along the hill. They followed the creek to a fork where another holler carried spring rain through the woods. Jim started climbing at an angle to the slope. The land rose steep to a rocky knob, and loose shale showered down from his boots. He waited on a ledge for Wayne and Clabe.

"Bad place to come on a bear," Clabe said.

"It's tracking panther," Jim said. "They favor cliff holes to live in."

Wayne spat and watched it fall sixty yards to the soft earth. "Cat ain't fit to eat," he said.

"It's not cat we're here for." Jim's voice was cold as a creek rock. "You two go that way. I'll sneak up on his other side. Clabe, you keep that rifle still. I want the first shot."

What happened after, there's no way to tell it nice. Many a man's got a hunting story and some make killing out to be fun. It ain't. It's easy and hard both at once, but one thing it's not is fun. It's just killing.

Jim climbed to the top and circled through brush. The dogs growled ahead of him. That bear was standing on its hind legs with its back against a big chunk of limestone. Its mouth hung wide and snarling, bloody fur matted below the chin, its front paws spread to hug or hit. The bear batted the bluetick so hard, it flew into a shagbark hickory and broke its back. Other dog jumped for the bear's throat but latched onto its shoulder instead. The bear fought fierce, trying to sling the dog off. Jim came in close. Straight across the knob from him, Clabe leaned against a tree to steady his aim. He was hid by shadows, and waiting on Jim to shoot first.

Jim aimed real careful but the bear dropped to all fours. Jim's shot went over the bear and hit Clabe, who went down like a stuck hog. Wayne fired his pistol six times. Shot the dog. Shot the tip of the bear's nose off. Other four bullets rattled tree leaves back through the woods. Bear reared again, mad.

Jim got his rifle loaded and this time he hit that bear square in the heart. It lit down and moved towards Jim, who stood there, reloading. Bear was going slow and bleeding mean. Jim laid the gun barrel right against the bear's eyeball. He shot and the woods got real quiet. For a long spell there wasn't a blown leaf to be heard. Jim started in laughing and pretty soon it turned into tears and he was crying. He laid smack on that bear's humped-up back and cried worse than a child pushed off tit by a new baby.

The top of the rock was a mess with dogs, bear, and men laying thick in the dirt. Clabe was shot through the back of his arm and into his side. Arm muscle had slowed the bullet down some. He told Wayne to make sure and get the baby's head. Wayne nodded, holding his brother's hand.

Jim slit the bear's throat. He went to the broke-back dog whimpering in the brush and cut its throat. Then he moved to Wayne and Clabe.

"Stay away from him," Wayne said. "It ain't that bad."

"Bear get him, too?"

"You shot him."

"I never."

"We done what we come for," Clabe said. "Patch this hole in me and let's get to the house."

The ball had hooked around a rib and wasn't too hard for Jim to pry out. He stuck a pinch of gunpowder in the wound. He took the flint from his gun and sparked it, and the powder burnt the bullet hole shut. Black smoke rose from Clabe's shirt. He passed out cold.

It was close to dark and they had to get off the cliff

while they could still yet see. Wayne went to the bear and gutted it like a deer. A stink blew out. He wiped his palms in dirt so the knife wouldn't slide from his grip. He found the belly-bag, pulled it out, and sliced it open. Inside was a dark lump the size of a squash. Wayne tucked it in the gunnysack tied to his waist.

"If you're hunting fresh liver," Jim said, "save me the heart."

Wayne gagged and turned away.

Clabe's arm was tied to his chest and he'd woke up. Jim helped him sit, then looked at Wayne. "Skin that bear and we'll use its hide to keep Clabe warm. He takes a fever, he's done."

"You," Wayne said.

Jim shrugged and squatted over the bear, knife drawn. He skinned fast, ripping the hide in three or four places. He didn't worry with the legs, but ripped out a big patch from neck to rump, and covered it with leaves to soak the blood. A caterwauling echoed up the rock and into the woods. It was a wailing moan, like a person hurt bad. As one scream died, another began. Night was coming fast.

"Dog me blind," Jim said. "Panthers."

Those boys were in a fix and the panther screams rang like a dinner bell. Evening star hung bright as metal. It was the old of the moon and there wasn't much light to see by. Good time to plant crop, but not walk panther cliffs at night. In an hour it'd be full dark. Jim loaded his flintlock. He had enough powder for one long shot or a couple of short ones. Clabe breathed hard, wrapped in bear hide. His muzzle-loader lay beside him.

Jim started dragging the bear and Wayne helped him

push it off the cliff into the gray dusk. Then they tossed the two dead dogs. The panther noise quieted. Wayne and Jim got Clabe on his feet and they went down the west side of the cliff. There wasn't no easy to it. That side was steeper but it put the hill between them and the panthers. Jim led. He moved crossways along the slope, using scrub pines to hold his weight. They were on a skinny ledge above a cliff, the worst part of the hillside. After that, the land sloped out gentle. The last of the sun lit the rock.

Shale crumbled beneath Clabe's foot, and the arm tied to his body ruined his balance. Wayne grabbed for him and a tuft of bear fur came away in his hand. Clabe fell halfway down the cliff, his gun clattering. He grabbed hold of a scraggly bush on a narrow outcrop. The bear hide flapped and a panther stepped from the woods, tail longer than its body. Clabe looked up.

"Lost my gun," he yelled.

"You're all right," Jim called.

Wayne spoke quietly. "I'll climb down to him."

"Panther'll beat you," Jim said.

"Kill it then."

Jim squatted awkwardly and propped the flintlock over a knee. He sighted on the panther. Its belly was pressed down, the head sunk low, and the end of its tail twitched. Wind blew the bear hide and the panther froze. Jim aimed at the flat top of its head. He fired and that panther thrashed backwards and didn't move.

"What are you shooting at?" Clabe yelled.

"Hush up," Jim said. "Talking'll sap you."

Jim braced the gun across his legs and fished out a scrap of wad and another lead ball. He tamped it in the barrel with a ramrod. Wayne stretched one leg down the cliff.

"Don't try it," Jim said. "You'll fall, too. Only way to get him is from below. You'd have to climb up to him, and lower him down with a grapevine. Then both of us pack him on home."

"I'll do it," Wayne said.

"Take too long."

"I got time."

"He don't," Jim said. "Yonder comes the mate."

Another panther walked from the tree line, thin shoulders bunched around a stretched neck. It moved to the base of the cliff, watching the bear hide. Three half-grown cubs followed it close. Right there was a good time for a praying man to pray, and a man today would have set to it. Those boys then knew God better. He'd made panther same as he made us. People now want animals to have the same rights as a man, but back then it was the other way around.

"They ain't had no meat all winter," Jim said. "About like you and me."

"Shoot it," Wayne said. "Shoot them all."

"I only got one shot worth of powder left."

Wayne stared at his brother hunched against the rock, holding tight to the shrub. Clabe couldn't see the panthers, didn't know the one was coming along the slope. The bush shook and dust sifted down.

"Clabe," yelled Wayne. "What're you doing?"

"This bush has got the sweetest gooseberries I ever did taste. I'll save you some."

"Eat all you want."

"Wayne," said Jim. "It'll be too dark to see in a minute."

"Let him finish."

Jim used the last of his powder to load the gun. It wasn't up to him. He'd done what he came for and Wayne had helped him. Now he'd stick by Wayne. After a few minutes, the shrub stopped shaking. Fifty feet away, the panther climbed to higher ground and stopped, watching Clabe.

"Wayne," said Jim. "It's on you to say. I'm just married in, but he's your brother. You got to tell me."

The big cat was still climbing. When it got above Clabe, it would wait till dark and jump. The cubs were near behind. Their winter-thick hides were leaking hair, snagged by rock and brush.

"He sure did love to fish," Wayne said. "Finest brother I ever had."

Jim wiped sweat from his hands and bent his face over the rear sight. "Best not look," he said.

"I got to."

"Don't."

Wayne shut his eyes and turned his face to the cool rock. He squeezed the piece of bear hide tight. A breeze moved along the cliff and when it stopped blowing, the gunshot came. The sound bounced against the rock and echoed down the holler, then returned, and faded away. Wayne looked down. The big panther was in a crouch, staring up the cliff where sparks had flashed from the gun barrel. Clabe lay very still. He'd never move again.

"It's done," Jim said. "Come on."

Well, they made it off that rock without more fuss.

It was full black dark and they were lost, bad lost. Wayne set off leading. Hit a little creek, followed it to a fork, and climbed the hill. He walked that ridge to a holler, went down into it and four hours later they were out. Wayne brought them home and he'd never been in those woods before. He couldn't say how he done it. People said the baby's head told him where to go, whispered to him all night long.

The whole creek showed up for the double funeral. They never found enough of Clabe to bother with digging a hole. Rose's grave was the littlest you ever did see.

That place got to be called Shawnee Rock and people stayed away. Wouldn't hunt, fish, or log over in there. My grandpaw said there were two spirits to it. Said one was an old bear looking for its hide. Other was a fat man hunting his gun.

About forty years ago I set off walking out Flatgap Ridge. I aimed to go where the bear killed the baby, then sleep on Shawnee's top. Back then I was plumb bold. Hit the ridge at midday and it was full of roses. I mean roses. You could haul off bushel baskets full and not see no less. Every one of them roses was cocked like a dog's ear, looking at me. I left out of there and never did go back.

Today's kindly cool with the sky mason-jar blue, gray at the edges like a lid. Winter'll close down hard soon. Bear and panther were all killed off in Grandpaw's day. In mine, we cleared out the bobcat and coyote. My sons were left with snakes to kill. The hills are safe now but folks still leave. At night there's not so many stars as used to be. Some might say I'm old and getting squirrely but they ain't nobody living close by to judge myself against. I'm going to bed.

———

Cody listened to the tape recorder humming in the silence. Night had spread across the land and into the house, and he could see the humped outline of Tar Cutler dead beneath the quilt. Cody ejected the cassette. He glanced again at Tar, expecting him to lean forward and grin at the prank. A mouse scurried along Tar's stiffened arm.

Drops of rain rustled leaves outside, thudding against the sheet metal roof. Water dripped through the ceiling and landed in a bucket, loud as a pistol shot. Cody stood sideways in the door, not wanting to look at the bed, afraid to turn his back on the corpse. Everything was wrong. He ran to the yard and placed the tape on an oak chopping block. A hickory-handled ax leaned against it.

"The wicked shall be cut off in darkness," Cody muttered.

He raised the ax and brought it down hard, scattering shards of plastic. He chopped and chopped until his arms were weary and the noise of the ax died away in the drizzling rain. Thunder rumbled low along the hilltops. He lifted his chin, panting, the ax dangling from his hand. He'd never felt so full of God's glory.

A breeze brought Tar's smell from the open door. Cody covered his nose. If he waited in the house while the storm passed, the low pressure and humidity would make the smell unbearable. He hurried along the dark path, his flashlight a dull gleam against the woods.

Halfway out the ridge, lightning hit a tree above his head. After a few seconds the lightning shot from the ground in front of him, having followed the tree to a root and struck a buried rock. Cody dropped the ax and began running down the steep hill. Branches tore at his face and he fell, tumbling in the dark. The flashlight shattered. He crawled to a hickory and crouched in its shelter.

Lightning cracked again, and in the sudden light Cody thought he saw movement in the woods. When the next quick flash came, he realized he'd gone down the back side of the hill and was hiding in the shadow of Shawnee Rock. He shivered, jaw tight. He pulled the small red Bible from his pocket and opened it. Rain began dissolving the glue that bound the pages to the spine. Wet paper flew like tissue in the wind. Cody trembled on his knees, watching the pages vanish in the darkness.

Wind and thunder bellowed above him. He curled his body around the tree trunk. The top was jerking wildly, and he could feel the roots pull from the earth. The ground was lifting beneath his body. A gust yanked the hickory from the soil, tipping Cody along the slope. He rolled onto his back and saw the heavy trunk falling toward him. A Bible page was plastered to the bark. Cody closed his eyes. He wished he had some whiskey and a gun.

SMOKEHOUSE

Fenton leaned against the icy wind that rushed up the hollow, trapped by the steep hillsides. He clamped his teeth, trying not to shiver. Blown snow lay like a shawl across his shoulders. His right molars were throbbing and he wondered if the gold bridge in his mouth contracted with the cold.

The wind slid away, replaced by the eerie cry of a coyote. After the mines shut down and people left, the coyotes had begun coming home. There'd been several sightings and two shot dead last fall. Fenton had never seen one, though he'd heard they were scruffy wild dogs, not good for much. Wind followed him into the barn, swirling hay in tiny funnels, that slowly settled as he closed the heavy door. He sank his arm into a crib full of knobby feed corn so cold it crabbed his knuckles. Buried in a corner was a pint bottle and a rusted coffee can full of money.

His wife forbade his keeping whiskey in the house since her Melungeon blood made her willful. Melungeons lived deepest in the hills, were the finest trackers and hunters. They were already there when the European settlers arrived. Melungeons weren't black, white, or Indian, and they didn't know where they'd come from.

Fenton slipped the thick roll of money into his pocket. It was carefully garnered from autumn dealing at the Rocksalt Trade Day. He'd taken an ancient well pulley, claimed it an antique, and worked several swaps that included a wheelbarrow, two pistols, a VCR, fifteen railroad ties, a minibike with no seat, and a pair of billy goats. He'd turned it all to cash.

Fenton moved into the night that was paled by snow, and took a shortcut through the woods to Catfish's smokehouse. He'd made the trip hundreds of times, first as a kid, then as a young man, and now, he realized, as a man not quite old yet. Forty-four was a peculiar age. He didn't receive the respect of age but was denied the excuses of youth. Mainly he was better at doing things he'd always done, such as walking to the smokehouse for a night of fun. Winters seemed colder now and he wondered if that was a sign of getting old. He'd ask Catfish.

Dim light glowed through the tree line at the end of the ridge, then was gone. Someone had opened the smokehouse door. Fenton passed the rock chimney, all that remained of the old Gerald place, long since burned down. Instead of rebuilding, Catfish had moved into his in-laws' house. Fenton tucked the bottle in the chimney's hearth and walked to the smokehouse.

He knocked twice, said his name, and the door opened. Snow skittered inside, disappearing in the heat. Catfish stood grinning, a big man with a beard that didn't quite cover four scars on his right cheek. He'd smashed through a windshield at fifteen, but let people think he'd been cut by a knife. Fenton had spent more time with him than with his wife. They had mined together, hunted and fished year-round, and dragged each other home drunk in the old days. Catfish's beard was four years long.

"By God, boys," Catfish said. "Fenton must've shot his wife for her to let him out."

The other men laughed. Fenton removed his coat and leaned over the stove, converted from a fifty-gallon drum. The faint smell of pork still lingered in the smokehouse air. As kids, he and Catfish had nailed cardboard to the rough, ax-hewn stud walls. Over that they'd glued Wishbook pages that were now peeling away. Fenton nodded to the men sitting around a table lit by a Coleman lantern.

W. Power winked. He was a World War II veteran who raised hogs up Bobcat Hollow. He had been the square dance caller until TV reached the hills and people stayed home on Saturday nights. As oldest, he sat closest to the fire. Beside him slouched Connor. Once a month Connor went to Rocksalt with the purpose of going to jail. He'd been married and divorced three times, and now slept with other men's wives. Connor's features marked him pure Melungeon: high cheekbones, black hair, brown skin, and pale blue eyes. He was rat-tail skinny from eating diet pills.

Fenton was surprised to see Duke hunched at the table, his head low to his shoulders like a dog. Tonight was the first time he'd sat in their game. Many years ago there'd been trouble in the coalfields and Duke was arrested for defending his brother. The law gave Duke a choice: join the army or go to jail. He put in twenty-five years, and returned with a Vietnamese wife and no children. Duke was the same age as Fenton, and he wondered if Duke felt old or young.

"It's time, boys," Catfish said. "Dealer's choice. No wild cards. All bets of property have got to go by the players in the pot. First jack deals. Any guff?"

"Just one," said Connor. "You ever catch that guy?"

"Who?"

"Guy that stole your razor." He laughed until noticing that everyone was silent, then ducked his head and rubbed his hands rapidly together. "Cold as a well digger's ass, ain't it."

Fenton took the empty seat, two concrete blocks topped with a plank. Catfish flicked the cards face-up around the table. A jack showed at W.'s seat. He called seven-stud, and began to shuffle, his ancient, labor-thickened fingers awkward with the deck.

With an ace showing, Connor led the betting. Fenton folded after three cards to avoid the early enthusiasm that sent money across the table fast and loose. Duke peeked at his hole cards once and followed the deal with his eyes. Connor bet high, and Catfish and W. dropped out. Duke raised. After a minute of eyeballing, Connor called the raise.

"You ain't buying the first pot," Connor said. He flipped a pair of aces. "I got two bullets coming your way."

"Three fours wired," Duke said, showing his hand. "I never bluff on the last card."

He pulled the pile of greasy bills in front of him, no expression on his face. Connor slouched in the old maple chair and tucked a cigarette in the gap between his upper front teeth. When he talked, the cigarette didn't move but his legs jittered from the diet pills.

"Thought I had the pot and wound up sucking hind tit," he said.

"That's the way it goes," Duke said, "first your money then your clothes."

"Since I lost square, I'll not say you got a smart mouth."

"Best not," Duke said, his voice low. They stared at each other across the scarred table.

"Next case," Catfish said. "You two keep your panty hose on. I'd run you outside but it's a blizzard coming on. We'll be burning furniture soon."

He glanced at Fenton for help.

"I reckon I got the best seat, then," Fenton said. "Concrete don't burn good."

W. stood and fed a split oak log into the stove.

"I'll take my shift now," he said. "But it's on you pups to keep me warm. The old woman'll faint if I get carried home on a door. Happened to my uncle once."

"What?" Connor said.

"He died."

"Just the one time?"

W. cocked his head and skewered Connor with a stare.

"If it weren't for rheumatiz, arthritis, and outright pity for a tomcat, I'd black your eyes and send you home."

Everyone laughed and W. returned to the table, worn smooth at the edges from the combined hours of men's hands. The steel stove cooled. Connor spat on it, and when it failed to ball up and dance, he stood to add more wood. He placed a hand on W.'s shoulder.

"Stay rested, old man. Don't want you wore out before we fight."

"Honey, you'd best pack a lunch," W. said. "You'll need your strength."

The faint smell of old smoked meat increased with the heat. They played steadily for a few hours, each man accommodating to the rhythm of the game: three shuffles, a cut, the whisper of cards and money. Fenton's bridgework ached. One of the tiny struts had broken and he wiggled it with his tongue. His legs and feet felt frozen while his upper body sweated from the stove's uneven warmth. He was down three hundred, coming in second again and again with cards too good to fold. He tightened his play, hoping the others wouldn't notice and drive him out with raises he couldn't afford.

After losing a big pot to Duke, Connor stepped outside and returned with his face flushed by whiskey. Nobody drank inside. Three years ago Catfish had banned liquor after a scuffle that left a man shot in the forearm. Everyone dived to the floor except W. He insisted they play the hand before doctoring the wounded, and W. won with kings full. A day later someone shot the shooter's chimney off his roof, following the old Melungeon code of warning. Vengeance escalated until a man was killed and then another in retaliation.

Feeling responsible, Catfish shut down the game for six months. When he reopened, he barred guns and whiskey, and considered banning Melungeons. Fenton argued that Connor and W. claimed Melungeon blood and would take it the wrong way. Since Fenton's wife was Melungeon, he'd have to follow the ban as well. Catfish relented. He understood that loyalty to his friend meant preventing Fenton from having to choose a side.

Connor complained about bad luck and the weather. On his deal, the deck slipped from his hands.

"Too greasy," he said. "Where's the flour poke?"

Catfish handed him the bag he kept in a corner. Connor dumped the cards in, shook the bag, removed the deck, and dropped the cards again. Flour dappled the floor.

"Too slick, now," he said.

"Let Catfish deal for you," Fenton said.

Connor shrugged and passed the deck. Wind carried the high yip of a coyote along the ridge. Fenton had heard they never attacked humans, but he didn't trust any animal in the woods. He'd once strangled a coon that had chewed a hole in his tent on a fishing trip.

"Door locked?" Connor said.

Catfish nodded.

"Don't let that coyote spook you," W. said.

"Takes more than that."

"It should," W. said. "A coyote is on the human side of dog. Most mutts, they're to the dog side of a man."

Duke's mouth pulled at the corners. "That's the first good sense I heard since leaving Asia," he said.

Fenton glanced at Catfish to see if he understood.

"Wood sure is handy for burning, ain't it," Catfish said. "Be a hard night without it."

Wood was a favored topic, with each man having a preference, depending on season and purpose. Fenton took a breath, intending to explain the virtues of pine, useless in a stove, but sure to draw furious opinion. Duke spoke first. "It's not wood that burns."

Wind shivered the door, rattling the hinges. Stray snowflakes fluttered through a crack and specked the floor. Catfish began to shuffle.

"Let's throw out the log pile, then," he said. "If wood don't burn, we'll get some elbow room in here. Place ain't big enough to swing a cat in."

"Oxygen burns, not wood," Duke said.

Fenton frowned at the stove, which was flaking paint from the heat. He'd burned wood all his life and enjoyed watching a log's collapse into fine gray ash.

"Then where's the wood go?" he said.

"Gets took hostage till the heat shows up," Connor said. "To hear him tell it, I don't reckon a hen lays eggs either."

"Not without a rooster," Duke said. "And that's what wood is. Oxygen is a hen and fire's the egg."

His voice held a tone of finality that silenced the men. Fenton didn't know if Duke was joking or presenting fact. Maybe he'd learned something in his years away, or maybe his sights were a little off.

Connor kneaded his crotch with both hands.

"If that's true," he said, "I got me a big old log need-ing a hen. I'll bet twenty dollars against five I got the stoutest here."

The men grinned, shaking their heads. Connor leaned close to W.

"I heard you owned a turkey neck, old man. Willing to put money on it?"

W. rubbed the side of his nose. The red-veined tip hung nearly to his lip. Patches of white hair showed under his jaw where he'd missed while shaving.

"It hibernates come winter. Catch me at the thaw if I'm still living." He jerked his chin at Catfish. "Deal, son. I ain't had a hand in ten years."

The men laughed and everyone anted but Duke, who stared across the table at Connor.

"Maybe I got what you're after," Duke said. His head was tipped forward, mouth tight, eyes hard. He snapped a five-dollar bill between his hands. "I'll take your bet."

Connor snatched a bill from his pile and set it to the side.

"You first," Connor said.

"No. I called your bet."

Connor lifted his eyebrows to Catfish.

"Way it is, Connor," Catfish said. "It's on you to show your hand."

Saliva clung to the corners of Connor's mouth. He pushed his lower jaw left and scratched it, frowning. Fen-ton recognized the gesture from previous card games. Con-nor's bluff had been called and he wanted to fold, but he'd proved himself so many times, he was stuck in the habit.

A knot exploded in the stove, rattling the metal like

buckshot. Connor scooted his chair away from the table, slowly stood and turned around. The back of his belt loosened and his jeans went slack. His right arm pumped twice. Fenton sucked the inside of his cheeks to stifle his laugh. Connor was cheating with a couple of strokes. Suddenly he spun back, his genitals swinging at the dusky edge of the lantern's light.

Duke's hands lay across his eyes.

"You win," he said. "I fold."

"You never looked." Connor's face turned red as he quickly stuffed and zipped his pants. "I don't know what to say about a man who makes a bet and don't look at the cards."

Duke uncovered his eyes and gazed steadily at Connor.

"Now I know how you play."

Wind rushed beneath the old smokehouse, carrying the smell of char up from cracks in the floor. Cigarette smoke rose to the high side of the slanted ceiling.

"My dead uncle's was bigger," W. said.

Connor spun his chair to straddle it backwards, legs splayed around the ladder back. His eyes were grim. Catfish dealt, naming the cards in a loud voice.

"Hook to the Duke. Connor gets a nine. A queen for Fenton." He flipped an ace to himself. "The doctor, always good to see." He bet without looking at his hole cards. "Five in the dark."

Everyone called and Catfish moved the cards smoothly across the table.

"Ten to the nine, straightening. Two diamonds for the Duke. Fenton gets a six." Catfish gave himself a second ace. "Another doctor, got to bet ten on the clinic."

Fenton's up cards matched his hole to give him two pair early. He raised the limit. Everyone called but W. "I got a hand like a foot," he said, and turned his cards over.

After the next round, Catfish bet twenty and Connor called. Fenton raised sixty-four dollars, knowing that unusual bets threw Connor out of kilter; he wasn't so sure about Duke. Both men called and Catfish dropped out. The last up card didn't help Fenton. Connor got an eight to give him four to a straight showing. Duke's card was a fourth diamond. He passed the bet to Connor, who grinned as he counted a hundred into the pot. Fenton studied the cards. He'd need a full house to beat the straight and the flush. The pot was worth the bet, but his cards weren't. Fenton sighed and pushed money to the center of the table. He was tired and ready to quit, and hoped it wasn't because of age. Duke silently called the bet.

"River card," Catfish said. "Read them and sleep."

Duke refused to look at his final card. He stared at Connor for a long time and asked how much money he had in front of him.

"Hundred and eighty," Connor said.

"Then the bet is three eighty." Duke counted money, slow and careful for all to see.

Connor rubbed his face with both hands. He lit a cigarette and examined his hole cards, chewing his lower lip. The cigarette burned unsmoked between his fingers. A couple of minutes passed in which Duke still did not look at his last card. Connor cracked his knuckles, a sound like green wood in a fire.

"Call, raise, or fold," Catfish said.

"Are you in this?" Connor said.

"It's your bet's all."

"I don't need no tips on how to play."

"Then do it and keep your mouth off me."

Connor tipped his chair on its back legs and slipped his hands behind his head.

"Boys," he said. "I'm trying to give the man a chance to look at his hand. I was raised right, not like some."

Duke pressed his forefinger on his final card and slowly pushed it into the center of the table beneath the pile of cash. He pulled his hand back empty.

"Maybe I don't need it," he said. "Maybe all I need is your bet."

"I'm shy two hundred," Connor said.

"You could raise me your truck."

The skin of Connor's face paled as he glanced at the door, on the other side of which sat his pickup. He studied Duke's four diamonds and fingered his money. With shaking hands Connor turned a hole card to show his straight. His voice was sharp and disgusted.

"I'm out," he said. "First good hand all night and goddam if I don't run into a diamond flush."

"Girl's best friend," W. said.

"Shut up, old man. What you know on girls won't fit up a gnat's ass."

"I been married fifty-one years, to a woman."

Fenton's last card was worthless, leaving him with the two pair. He began counting diamonds. He'd seen seven and Duke was showing four more, which left two for the flush. Duke hadn't bet early. He'd been fishing then, and Fenton realized it was a bluff. Duke had nothing. If Fenton won, he'd be even for the night.

"I call," Fenton said. He was fifteen dollars short. "And raise."

He reached in his pants for a pocketknife. It was old and not worth much, but still his favorite. He snapped the blade open. Duke shook his head, refusing the property bet.

"This ain't it," Fenton said.

He slowly lifted the knife and slid the blade into his open mouth, below the bridge. He squinted, blinking when the tiny strut pulled from his gum. He pried the entire bridgework loose and tossed the shiny wet gold on the table. The knife's tip held a drop of blood that he wiped on his pants.

"Jesus God," Duke said. "If I raised back, I guess you'd bet a finger."

He turned his cards face down and pushed the money across the table. Connor stood, clattering his chair to the floor. His pupils were barely rimmed by iris. He swayed for a moment, trying to speak.

"The house?" he finally said. "You got a full house?"

"You don't want to know," Fenton said.

Connor flipped Fenton's cards to show his hand.

"Two pair," Connor said. His upper lip rose, showing teeth the size of soup beans. "That's my pot," he said.

Duke's voice came hard and mean.

"Stay off that money."

Connor jerked his head wildly, settling on W.

"Old man," he said. "You going to set and let them railroad me? You against me, too?"

"It's only a game," W. said. "Folding a winner's good poker. Makes up for all the losers a man stays in on."

Connor pivoted and kicked his chair. A rung broke and he continued to kick until the dry maple lay in pieces. The floor shook and rafter dust sifted down. When Connor was finished he snatched a chair leg, turned and snarled. No one moved. He stepped to the door and pushed it open. Cold air rushed into the smokehouse, causing the hole in Fenton's gum to ache.

"I ain't forgetting this," Connor said. "I ain't forgetting how you run me out. Every damn one of you."

He walked into the glittering darkness of the snow. Wind smacked the door, pinning it to the outside wall. Cards and money blew off the table to mix with the wreckage of the chair. Fenton watched the edges of a five-dollar bill blacken against the stove. Catfish closed the door. No one looked at each other.

Fenton walked around the room collecting money from corners like hunting mushrooms. Three kicks made the door rattle. Duke picked up a thin log and moved to a corner. Connor stood outside, refusing to enter. A stripe of snow clung to the right side of his body.

"Won't start," he said. "Who's got cables?"

"I walked," Fenton said.

"Me and W. came with Duke," Catfish said.

Duke turned from the stove. "In the trunk." He pushed a hand in his pocket for keys.

"Keep them," Connor said. "I ain't owing you nothing."

"It's hardly owing," Duke said. "Winter's winter."

Connor spoke to Catfish. "I'll borrow some kindling, if you ain't caring."

Catfish loaded Connor's outstretched arms and closed the door. The room was cold again.

"Somebody better help him," Fenton said.

No one moved, and Fenton put on his coat. Outside, snow hit him at a hard slant. He raised a shoulder and tipped his head, walking at an angle to the wind. Snow blew like vapor across the ground, squeaking beneath his boots.

Connor was jacking the front of his truck, cursing steadily. He spun with a pistol in his hand.

"It's me," Fenton said.

"There's a goddam coyote out here," Connor said. "First I ever seen one. Big as a hound dog."

"Need a hand?"

"I don't need nothing." He plunged the lever down, the jack clicking loud. "Cables won't do any good. The block's froze up." He switched hands. "I never did see a truck that didn't pick the worst time to break down. My whole life I've worked on cars at zero weather with no goddam gloves."

The front bumper was two feet off the ground.

"Ought to do her," Fenton said.

Connor twisted newspaper into rolls and placed them beneath the engine block. He laid a few twigs over the paper, built a tepee of bigger sticks. "Block the wind, will you," he said.

Fenton squatted beside him, feeling the cold slice through his coat. Connor struck three matches until the paper caught. He worked the fire carefully, making air holes at the bottom and maneuvering sticks over the burning twigs. Snow turned to water on the front of his coat. He used the biggest branch to make a torch, which he moved in circles around the metal.

"She'll start now," he said.

He climbed into the cab. The pickup rocked but remained on the jack, and the engine caught on the second try. He swallowed two pills from a plastic bottle in the glove box.

"Give me a lift," Fenton said.

The road led past his house and he wanted to make sure Connor went home. Connor had already served thirty days for assault and the county judge didn't like him. He'd made it clear that Melungeons should stay where they belonged.

"You'd better walk," Connor said. He patted the pistol beside him on the seat. "Could be I ain't headed straight home."

He eased the clutch until the jack fell and the front wheels bounced in the fire, scattering sparks. The pickup blurred into the gray air. Fenton stomped the fire, wondering if he should warn Duke. He didn't much care for him but nobody deserved a bushwhack. Telling him betrayed Connor, but it might also stop him from killing a man. Fenton shuddered. He trudged to the old chimney and dug his bottle from the bricks. Connor was a lot of talk and maybe this was more of it.

Fenton capped his bottle, returned to the smokehouse, and opened the door. A wave of heat stung his face. W. and Duke were passing a flask.

"Game's over," Catfish said. "Want a drink?"

Fenton shook his head.

"Shut that damn pneumonia hole," W. said. He placed a gnarled hand on Duke's leg. "You know this pup's part Melungeon on his mama's side. By God, I knew it, by God."

"Thought you'd be off counting your winnings," Duke said to Fenton.

"I broke even."

Duke laughed and patted W. on the back. "If old W. would loosen up and take a chance, he might be the big man."

"Way I see it," W. said, "you don't have much bragging room."

Duke smiled a hard, tight-lipped smile. "All I lost was money." He poured whiskey into the flask lid and drank it, staring at Fenton. "I got all my teeth and nobody saw my wiener. I won what counted."

The money felt heavy in Fenton's pockets, like wet insulation that let weather in. He decided to give Connor's back to him, but not tonight, when Connor was somewhere waiting on the road, trigger finger tucked in his armpit to keep it warm.

"Be leaving," Fenton said. At the door, he turned to face Duke. "Watch your chimney."

Tree limbs crackled in the woods, tightening in the frigid air. Pale breath clouded around him. He'd walked home a loser many times, feeling bad. The times he'd won felt just as bad for taking money from his friends. Tonight, breaking even was the worst of all.

He started downhill and his foot skidded on frozen moss. He grabbed a sapling and the wood broke, stiff and fragile from the cold. Fenton twisted, flailing his arms and falling backwards over the steep hill. He watched the snow-laden treetops give way to black sky. His head struck a rock.

He was not sure how long he'd been lying on his

back but he was cold, very cold. Snow beaded on his face. His head hurt and he wondered if anything was broken. He turned his head to check his neck. It still worked. A coyote stood just beyond arm's reach, shaggy fur ruffled around its head. Fenton lifted a stiff knee and the coyote growled, a low sound like a motor deep in a mine. It backstepped into shadows.

Fenton crawled to a tree farther up the slope and used it to stand. The wind was slower now and he wondered how long he'd been out. Neither knee worked well. He fell again, and realized that he couldn't make it home.

He stood and began walking, unsure if he was lifting his feet because he could no longer feel them in his boots. Sweat turned to ice on his forehead. He left the woods and headed for the dark shadow of the smokehouse. Leafless trees threw gray shadows across the snow. A car engine sputtered twice before cranking loud along the ridge. Duke's taillights flashed like animal eyes on the snowy road.

Fenton limped to the smokehouse and beat on the crossbar lock, surprised to see blood on his hand since nothing hurt. When the latch slid free, he stepped inside and closed the door. The fire was out.

He draped his body over the stove, pressing his hands against its warm underbelly, and stayed that way until the pain arrived and he could control his fingers. He banked the few glowing coals with a broken chair rung. He needed smaller kindling, but Catfish had given it all to Connor. Fenton dropped a playing card in. It burned feebly at the edges, the plastic coating releasing a black smoke until the tiny flame died. Fenton opened the bottle and sipped, hurting his chapped lips. He gasped as whiskey ran into the space where his bridge had been.

He searched his pockets for something to burn and found a used tissue matted into a frozen ball. He remembered his mother ironing his father's handkerchief Sunday morning before church. When the iron hit a wrinkle of dried mucus, it crackled from the heat. Fenton emptied his pockets, finding nothing.

From the direction of the road came two quick pistol shots, sharp and clear in the night. There was no answering gunfire. Fenton touched the back of his head and found blood clotted over a wound. The cold had probably stopped the bleeding early, and he wondered if the shot man had been so lucky. Connor had never been much of a hunter, plus he was hopped up. Fenton decided he'd probably missed.

On the table, Fenton divided his winnings into piles of ones, fives, and tens, hoping the ones would be enough. Newer bills, folded lengthwise, worked the best. Twice he had to warm his hands against the fading heat of the stove. His fingers were black and smoking but didn't hurt.

He blew on the embers and when they stayed orange he quickly arranged the folded dollars in the coals, laid two chair rungs like a grate, and placed a split log on top. The paper turned crisp and curly and finally flared. He could smell the old varnish burning off the rungs. Fire moved along the bark. There were four logs left, enough to get through the night.

He felt very old and realized that being forty-four meant knowing what not to do. Twenty years before he'd have waited with Connor. Maybe in another twenty, he'd warn Duke straight out. Fenton stretched on the floor, then curled on his side, facing the stove. His wife would call Catfish's wife in the morning, just as their mothers had called each other when they were kids. He closed his eyes. Catfish would come for him.

BLUE LICK
■■■■■■■■■■■■■■■

The funny-talked lady gave me a ten-page test that like to drove me blind marking in little circles no bigger than a baby catfish eye. When I was done, she said I was precocious. Then she called me a poor dear and I got mad on account of Daddy telling me never to let nobody say we were poor. He said to fight them if they did. I put my fists up fast. She saw how mad I was and asked me whatever for in that funny-talked way of hers.

I told her and she said, "I don't mean poor like that, there's other ways." She just set and looked at me, real pale like she never got out much. On her back was a new flannel shirt, still yet with the folding marks not wore out. She wore red-laced shiny boots. I'd never seen a woman wear blue jeans before unless it was somebody's granny but she wasn't that old. I put my fists back down.

She kept looking at me like I was some kind of black snake that you ain't supposed to kill or the rats will eat you out. My daddy said he chopped a black snake in half when he was little, and his own daddy tied him to a bucket and lowered him down a well over killing it. Daddy seen stars and it full day. Down below it was blacker than a cow's insides, and the brick well walls were slick as a glass doorknob. He said they've got glass ones down to the courthouse. Daddy ought to know because he's been there plenty, which is why I took them precocious tests anyhow.

She wasn't a state lady and she wasn't from town. She was a VISTA lady that got sent here over me and my brother, who can't talk plain. He can't say his Rs or his Ls, and there's some sounds he don't even know. I'm the one to understand him most. He ain't precocious. What he is, is a singer, singing made-up stuff. Daddy calls him Little Elvis.

That lady, she went and reached her hand over mine and it was the smoothest thing, smoother than a horse's nose hole, which is pure soft. She held my hand like you do a frog when you're fixing to cut its legs off and eat them. I let my fingers lay real still so they wouldn't wiggle and give her no big ideas. Mommy always did say I was full of big ideas. She took off two summers back and we ain't seen hide nor hair of her yet. Daddy used to say "fuck you bitch" to her and that was one of my brother's songs till we went to live with Granny on the Blue Lick River. Granny filled my brother's mouth full of lye soap over that song. He never liked her after that. He called her the fuck-you-bitch when she was far enough away, like out back at the toilet by the river. Granny goes in there at least a hundred times a day. She's skinny as a broom straw.

Daddy got out of prison early over there not being nobody to raise us up but Granny, who's old as God. The funny-talked lady asked if I knew why Daddy went to prison the first time. I knew all right. Daddy'd told us a million times about wrecking his car and waking up thinking he was dead. What he done was run his car ninety miles an hour off the road by a Shell gas station and plow through a fence into a horse. He woke up and the horse had come in the windshield on Daddy, covering him with blood that he thought was his own. A tree was blocking the *S* off the Shell sign. Daddy said he seen them big red letters and knew right then he'd died and gone to where everybody always said he'd wind up anyhow. The horse's belly had tore open and half a colt was hanging out with its legs on the floorboards. Daddy thought he'd turned into part goat, like the devil.

They locked him up a year because the man whose horse it was didn't like losing two at once. Daddy said he wouldn't have a record if he'd had the sense to hit a mare that wasn't knocked up. Plus the car was a borrowed car. When the man he borrowed it off heard how he run through a pasture fence into a horse, the man claimed it wasn't borrowed after all. He took to watching out for us when Daddy was in prison. He watched good, I reckon, because Mommy took off with him. After Daddy got out of La Grange, the man's barn burned down and people said it was Daddy done it, but nobody told the law.

Daddy came home with two tattoos on him right

smack over his titties. One said "Blue" and the other said "Lick." Little Elvis wrote on his ownself with an ink pen and Daddy laughed like a wild man when he seen it. You couldn't read what was wrote. It wasn't even letters, more like worm tracks on the riverbank.

Daddy's feet stunk bad, too. He said it was from wearing shoes all the time in La Grange, even in the shower and bed. Little Elvis started wearing his shoes to bed, but Granny said it made the sheets bad to be muddy, and Daddy took her side because there wasn't no mud in the joint. He said they had boys like girls in prison, too. Little Elvis wanted to know if their feet stunk. Daddy said we'd know we were grown-up men when our feet had a good solid stink to them. Little Elvis wanted Daddy's socks so he could hurry it up, but Daddy said that was bad luck and we'd have to find another way.

Little Elvis wanted bad to be a man and I started thinking on all the things that's got a smell to them. Grasshopper piss for one. Polecats and rotten eggs. Road kill, too, but I didn't feel like fooling with dead stuff. A boy that used to live down here did, and the state took him for cutting them animals up. He made his sister show me her thing once if I'd give him a bat my daddy killed that got in the house. After seeing her poon, I wanted that bat back. I just know he cut it up.

The only other thing I could think of was the toilet shack, which Granny called the White House. She planted honeysuckle around it to cut the smell but it drew mud daubers big as tree frogs. Me and Little Elvis went to the woods mostly. He used poison vine to wipe with once and never did wipe again after.

A month ago, I had to go bad and it was nighttime, with the moon not up yet. I sneaked out to a pine where the dead brown needles below was soft and would cover the smell up. Daddy was off fox hunting and everybody else in the world was asleep but me and it felt fine, just fine, being in the woods alone at dark. Then the hunting dogs got on my trail and started howling. I had to climb that pine, getting stickered by needles every branch. Dogs were barking below the tree, trying to claw their way up the trunk. There's not a dog in all creation that climbs trees. That's why trees are here, Daddy said, to give varmints somewhere to get away to.

Them dogs wouldn't leave and I had to do my business so bad it was hurting. I got scared it would back up in me like a culvert in a storm. What I did was just go ahead and go. First I pulled my pants down and kindly hung on to the tree and let my hind end aim through limbs I wouldn't have to climb back down on. I cut loose and the dogs jumped like somebody'd set them on fire. They were catching it in the air and eating it and then jumping again. Pretty soon they were fighting over scraps and I couldn't get my pants up on account of needing both hands to hold on to the tree with.

The men were coming out the ridge and I heard them arguing over whose dog was at the lead, and whose fox it was. Somebody shined a flashlight on me while the others pointed guns. They started laughing. One man said to Daddy, "I told you that dog was a shit-eating dog, he's treed your boy."

Daddy stepped right up to the man and said, "You wouldn't say such if I weren't on parole." Daddy put his gun down and looked around at all the men and said, "If he shoots me, tell the law I didn't have a gun." Then he hauled off and hit that man square in the face and knocked him back in the brush.

Daddy started kicking dogs off the tree trunk until there wasn't none left. The men were cussing, trying to sort dogs out. The man who Daddy had hit was whopper-jawed and he had his rifle in both hands pointed at Daddy. Daddy put his arms up. The other men were backing away. Daddy turned to the tree real slow, looked at me, and said, "Let go, damn it." I didn't want to, but I did. Pine branches scraped my face half clean off and Daddy caught me. He turned back to the man, holding me in front of him. The gun was aimed right at me.

"Your own boy," the man said.

He turned his gun and shot Daddy's dog. He went into the woods and he was gone, and all the others were gone, and Daddy let me down and we stood there in the dark while the hound dog sound got further away until there wasn't nothing to be heard since that shot scared everything in the woods. Daddy's best dog was dead, its throat blown out. He made me promise not to tell Granny how the dog got killed.

Because Little Elvis wanted to be a man, I took him out to the White House and we hung our feet down through the hole. He sang, "We're stinking our feet like old dead meat," over and over. Mud daubers had tunneled a nest in a high corner and I seen them but it was too late. They landed on Little Elvis's head and started biting and he tried to run, but forgot he was stinking his feet and fell through the hole. He grabbed hold of my legs. Then the mud daubers were on me and I screamed for Granny. She came out and said later she'd thought one of us had an eye poked out from all the hollering. She saw me half down the toilet hole and took me by the arm like I was laundry. Granny worked past me to snatch Little Elvis by the hair and haul him up, his head one red bump from mud dauber bites and his feet stinking all the way past his knees. Granny about busted the White House roof off laughing. She said Daddy fell in once when he was a boy, and Little Elvis thought that made it ok.

"In here?" he said. "Daddy fell in here?"

"No, it was a different place," Granny said.

What they did back then was move the White House when the hole filled up and she said Daddy's old hole was over where the turnips were growing now. Little Elvis got the idea that Daddy's feet stunk from turnips. He stomped them all summer, not leaving none to eat, and groundhogs got the mush. He'd lay in the dirt and sing, "Daddy's feet don't get burn up 'cause he mashed them in a turnip." The only way of keeping him out of the garden was tying him to the door but Granny's hands were too stiff and twisty for making good knots. I turned him loose every day.

By now we called Granny the fuck-you-bitch to her face because she locked us outside till dark, then made us take our clothes off and hose each other down before we could eat supper. We weren't allowed to wear anything in the house because of the dirt. All summer our shirt and pants laid outside overnight. Some mornings, we found Daddy laying out there, too. His head hurt so bad he had me water him with the hose. Little Elvis would sniff at Daddy's boots so he'd know man-smell against the time he was one. Daddy said we were a damn sure pair of stand-up boys.

When the sun moved over the ridge, he crawled to shade and along noon he'd light a cigarette and talk to us. "Shoot to kill," he said, "never wound. Fold a three-flush after five. Don't give women gifts. Always throw the first punch." Stuff like that he'd tell us, useful stuff that we were supposed to never let go of. I didn't, but Little Elvis can't remember much from day to day except food. Once he forgot how to ride a bike and I had to learn him all over again.

One day we found Daddy asleep in a car behind the house. He let us help him take it apart, and we threw hubcaps, headlights, and bumpers in the river. He un-screwed a quarter panel and put me and Little Elvis to tearing it up with tire tools. We beat and scratched until the car was stripped down like a go-cart and you could see how the gears worked. We broke all the glass out, too. Daddy stuck the big pieces in the back of his truck and drove away.

He came back with half-melted ice cream cones from Rocksalt and we ate what was left of them, looking at the car. Daddy said we could make a dune buggy of it. He'd drive us anywhere we wanted to go—wherever, we'd just go with sleeping bags, fishing rods, and night crawlers. We'd see the world living on fish and ice cream. And siphoning gas at night.

While we sat there watching the river, two police cars came to block our road. A big bald-headed cop told Daddy to sit on the grass while the short cop talked on a radio. Daddy didn't say nothing, he just sat. Two more cars showed up, not police cars but regular cars. The men weren't wearing cop suits but they acted like they were, and when one took his coat off against the heat, he had a pistol on a strap that went over his shoulders. He put the jacket back on when the bugs got to him. They're bad on the river but they don't bother me and Little Elvis because Daddy said we're river rats and mosquitoes know better than to fool with us.

The two cops who weren't cops had clipboards. They looked that car up and down with me watching and Little Elvis out front riding his bike and singing, "Police car squashed my daddy, police car squashed my daddy." He rode in a circle, which he's not good at, and kept wrecking until Daddy took him in his lap.

The man with the hid gun said, "It looks like the car all right." Then he asked me how long it was here.

"What," I said, "the river?"

He didn't like me saying that, which was fine by me because I didn't like him telling Daddy to sit under the tree. Not even Granny tells him what to do.

"We need a warrant," the other man said. "Nothing that kid says will do us any good."

He smiled at me the way I've seen teachers smile when they think I done something bad and they're pretending it ain't bad so I'll talk about it and they can give me a paddling. I got twelve licks once. Six for saying thank you when the teacher said I was wise, and six more for laughing after the first six licks. I had to laugh because I couldn't cry in front of everybody. Daddy said river rats never cry.

The men who weren't cops had that look on their face, like they wanted to give me a paddling but didn't have the reason yet.

"How long's this car been here, son?" the smiling one said.

I looked at him and then at the car, and I could hear Little Elvis singing.

"I ain't your son," I said.

The other man shook his head.

"That's my car," I said. "I'm putting it together. Daddy ain't helping or nothing. We're aiming to dune-buggy it on out of here."

One man laughed but the second one got that teacher look again, like he finally had his reason for a whipping.

"There's not a dune for a thousand miles any direction from here," he said.

When I told the funny-talked lady all this she said that's what she meant about precocious, how telling the cops that lie was precocious. I didn't like her knowing right off it was a lie because when Daddy heard me say it, he said it was the pure truth. The bald cop pulled out handcuffs and the short one said, "Not in front of his kids."

They made Daddy get in the back seat of the police car. They drove through the yard to the road, leaving big tracks in the grass and I wrecked my bicycle trying to catch up, bent the rim bad. I pushed it back to Little Elvis, who was sitting with his bike in a big mud hole. When I couldn't get him to come out, I sat down with him. We smeared mud on our faces and planned to break Daddy out and they'd not know who it was because of the mud.

The funny-talked lady grinned over that and said, "Some people don't always cooperate with people who can help. I hope you're not one of them."

I didn't say nothing and she asked if there was anything I needed. I'd never thought I needed anything but if she was asking, maybe there was. So I said, "To get Little Elvis back from the place the state put him."

I missed hearing him sing those songs even if they were dumb as ditch water. Many's the time I tried to make some up but they never came out right. Daddy always did say I sang like a combination lock, no key. It was Little Elvis who got the talent in our family, which was ok with me.

I wouldn't mind too bad talking to Daddy over that tore-up car business either. The owner was the same man whose dog treed me and who Daddy knocked down. I was the one who had to go and climb that pine and get the dog killed, Daddy locked up, and Little Elvis took.

I reckon Mommy'd never run off if I hadn't busted in on her and that neighbor man one night when I couldn't sleep for the racket they were raising. I screamed out, "You ain't my daddy." He looked at me back over his shoulder from where he was hunkered down in the middle of the bed like picking worms off tobacco and said, "Damn sure ain't, runt." He kicked me full in the head barefoot. Then he slapped Mommy in the jaw and I seen her naked buried under him with her hair in her face, and her eyes crazy.

"Go on and get," she said to me.

I ran out of the house, into the dark and way up a hillside. I didn't tell the funny-talked lady what it was I done up there that night, because what I done was hold off crying every which way. Jabbing a locust thorn in my hand worked best. Then Mommy and the man was gone and me and Little Elvis got moved to Granny's house, and Daddy was home for a summer. It was a good summer, too.

The funny-talked lady hugged me right then, just reached out and yanked me to her new-smelling flannel shirt and held me against her body. I tried to squirm away but it didn't do any good. She started in crying and that seemed like a good time to try and get a look down her shirtfront. After a while she said there was hope for me, she could save me. I told her I didn't want to be saved. Granny got saved four times, the last after Daddy went back to La Grange. Getting saved meant smiling at all the people who didn't like you, and they smiled back like they did.

The funny-talked lady closed her eyes and said she didn't mean church saved, there was more than one type of that, too. She said my test scores showed potential. I asked about Little Elvis. She didn't say anything and I could tell it was over not wanting to lie, because I used to do Granny the same way until finally I just went ahead and lied without the not wanting to getting in the way.

"What about him?" I said. "What about him?"

She put her hands on my shoulders and leaned her head to mine and looked right at me and talked quiet.

"You're it," she said. "You got all the potential for both of you. I'm afraid your brother is slow."

There's boys like that at school but Little Elvis wasn't like them. They're big and mean and can't even zip their own fly.

"You lie!" I yelled out, and tried to smack her, aiming for her face but only got her arm. She caught me and hugged me tight again, just like Mommy did the neighbor man when he hit her, and I did my best to look down her shirt until finally I gave it up. I just went and gave up everything and started crying. If they could take my daddy and my brother, they might as well take me away, too.

She turned loose of me and didn't say nothing but drove me on out the road to Granny's. She said she'd come by tomorrow. She tried to laugh, and said she'd bring some bug spray. I got out and walked in the tracks the tow truck had made dragging Daddy's borrowed car away. I couldn't stop thinking on Little Elvis, and I tried to make up a song about him but it wouldn't take. I went down on the riverbank and looked at the place where we'd thrown pieces of the car in at. There was nothing but river, not a rat in sight. I sat there till a mile past dark.

AUNT GRANNY LITH

Beth stood in shadows behind her nearest neighbor's house, listening to her husband's drunken laugh. Every fall was the same. Spring rain and summer sun gave a fine field of ear; late frost sweetened the crop. Casey traded half the liquor he made for supplies, and sold enough to fix the truck. His two-week bender brought him to Lil's.

Beth jerked the back door open and stepped through the cramped kitchen to the living room. Casey was slumped on the couch, a mason jar in his hand.

"Hell's bells," Lil said. "Will you look at what the dogs drug in."

"Want a seat?" Casey said.

"I'm not here on invite," Beth said.

"You sure to God ain't," said Lil.

"You know what I come for."

"Not selling Tupperware, I don't reckon." Lil tapped cigarette ash to the floor. "You ain't got much say in my house. Best be leaving while you still yet can."

"Have a drink, Beth," said Casey. "It's the awfullest good I ever did run."

"You got the jar lid?" Beth said.

"Somewheres."

"Put it on tight."

He patted his shirt pockets, then searched his pants. Lil scooted to the edge of the couch, her knees bent, ready to spring. She took a long pull on her cigarette. Her voice was sandstone harsh.

"Casey just might be tired of you."

"If you feel froggy," Beth said, "jump."

Lil flicked the lit cigarette at Beth and leaped from the couch, fingers hooked into claws. One hand twisted Beth's black hair. Both women stumbled across the room, knocking the stovepipe loose from the flue. Creosote dust drifted the air. Lil snatched the poker, slammed it hard against Beth's hip. Beth staggered, the low groan in her chest shifting to a growl. She spat in Lil's face, cocked her fist, swung. Her knuckles split against Lil's face and the poker clattered across the floor. Lil swayed like a tree at the final saw cut, mouth open, blank eyes blinking. As she fell, Beth gripped a handful of her long red hair and yanked. The hair tore loose, several strands still clinging to a chunk of scalp. Lil's head bounced. Her jaw was swollen and bloody.

"You won't bushwhack no drunks for a while," Beth said. "Leastways not mine."

She shoved the hair in her pocket and turned to Casey on the couch. His mouth hung open, his eyes half shut. She realized that he wouldn't have been much good to Lil, anyway. Beth yanked his shirt.

"Beth," he said.

"I'm here."

"My money's on you to clean her plow."

"Help me get you up."

"I can't get no upper."

Beth dragged him to the edge of the couch. Casey braced his arm around her shoulder, and she helped him out the front door. He pushed her aside. "You follow the hard way," he said, and tipped into the darkness, rolling down the slope, laughing and grunting. His arm smacked the truck door. "First here," he yelled. "Beth's on shotgun!"

She limped down the hill in moonlight glowing through the trees. Casey was a dark mound leaning against the truck. She rapped his nose with her fist.

"Pretty good lick," he said.

"Try and puke."

Casey shoved a finger down his throat.

When he finished, he wiped his mouth against the truck, and Beth coaxed him into the cab. She drove along the twin-rut road above the creek. Asleep against the dashboard, Casey looked angelic, his hands fisted into clubs. His face was broad as a coal shovel. A hard bump knocked Casey against her and he jerked the steering wheel. The pickup crashed down the hill, bounced over limestone, and plunged into the creek. Bullfrogs abruptly stopped their roaring.

Beth lit a match and leaned to Casey, who snored on the floorboards, short, thick arms pillowing his head. She opened the door and sank her foot into mud. The night sky was spattered white with stars. She found Orion and began walking just left of his lowest sword-star, ignoring the throbbing of her hip. Moonlight glistened on animal prints tipped by frost in the hardened mud. She followed the game path two miles to her property, bridled the mule, and draped Casey's logging chains over its back.

Thirty years before, Casey's first wife died the day after they were married. She'd been walking the property, scouting a garden place, and Casey found her beneath a tree with a broken branch piercing her face. It ran through her eye and into her brain. Casey married again. His second wife suffered a broken neck at the bottom of a steep cliff. Casey began carrying a pistol in his hip pocket, walking with an arm trailed back, hand hovering over the gun. He looked like a sideways-running dog.

A year later, while checking his crawdad traps on Lick Fork Creek, he saw Beth dipping water to carry home. Her denim workshirt clung to her body in damp patches. He offered to haul the buckets and she refused. The next day he came to court her on the front porch. Beth was the only daughter, the last child at home. Casey was the first man who ever made her laugh. When he left, Beth's mother came outside to sit on an upended washtub. Nomey built a cigarette, curled the end of her pants leg, flicked ashes into the cuff.

"What in case he wants to marry me?" Beth said.

"His people stick by theirs."

"They say he's hexed. Two wives done died on him."

"That boy's had a run of bad," Nomey said. "But he ain't full to blame."

"What is?"

"Hard telling."

"It still yet scares me."

Nomey gave Beth a piece of black moly root that she wore on a strip of leather tight above her hips. Two months later Beth announced her wedding. The local preacher refused to marry them, saying that he'd already sent two virgins to the grave and wouldn't risk another. Casey hired a preacher from Rocksalt.

Both families crowded the church. Two armed men guarded the door, and two more roamed the dusty parking lot. After the ceremony, several women stayed to pray for Beth, while the men escorted the newlyweds to the small house Casey had built. Beth's brothers carefully searched the house, the chicken house, and the hog pen. She watched them leave at dusk, firing guns into the woods. Casey's arm circled her waist.

"Whatever you want," he said. "It's yours. I got enough put by for a TV set."

"I got what I want," Beth said.

"You stay right by me, hear. There's a shotgun by the door and a pistol at the bed." He patted the buck knife on his hip. "This don't ever come off either."

Beth tipped her head and moved her mouth to his. She stood on her toes until he lifted. Her knees gripped him and he carried her through the living room to the small bed. They rattled it together for a long time.

After Casey was asleep, Beth felt the coarse of his beard stubble. She didn't know when it had grown. He'd shaved for the wedding, and his face had been smooth when they'd entered the house. She remembered her father's beard pricking her face when she was a child. She hadn't known him well before he died. Now she felt as if she knew him better.

She lay on her side admiring the dim outlines of her new house. She couldn't get used to the idea of being married. Nomey had told her it meant being loyal—to a certain point. If he hit her, he lost his claim. If he didn't come home once in a while, Beth could do the same, but she had to be careful. That sort of thing was harder for women than men. Nomey chuckled then and said that most things were, and that's why women were smarter than men. Beth had nodded, not quite understanding.

She rose from bed and looked through the window at the toilet shack above the creek. Come spring she'd lay flat rocks along the path and plant flowers. Beyond the shadowed hulk of a car, its rusted rims on cinder blocks, Beth saw someone scurry into the woods. She left the house and trailed the person to the head of the hollow, where the figure climbed an animal trail slanting up the slope and out the ridge. Beth followed half a mile before crouching behind a poplar to peek over the tree's lowest crotch. Sweat stung the brier scrapes on her face.

A nighthawk swooped to a halt on the ground. The figure bent, cooing to the bird. It was a small woman with ragged clothes, long hair, and shoulders that crooked forward. She crawled past the bird to a large log lying on the earth. She slipped into its hollow opening and the bird sat in front. The sky behind was empty.

Beth backtracked through the woods to the house. Casey was gone. An hour later the front door crashed open. He stood in the doorway, squinting against the light, his shotgun aimed at Beth, his other hand holding the pistol.

"Beth," he grunted.

He pointed the shotgun at the ceiling, carefully thumbing the hammers down. He slid the pistol in a jacket pocket.

"I ought to wear you out," he said. "Didn't I tell you not to go nowhere."

"I saw her, Casey. I followed her."

"Who?"

"I don't know."

Casey stared through the window, his shotgun poised.

"She's gone," Beth said. "Crawled into an old hollow log up on Flatgap Ridge. I thought she was a ghost."

"She might be."

"You know her?"

"Hope not."

"Who is she?"

"Tell me what you seen, Beth."

She sat in a rocking chair built by her grandfather, the wedding gift from her mother. She pushed the chair back and forth to form the rhythm for her words. When she finished, Casey's face was white as birch. His arm veins swelled from squeezing the shotgun, trying to stop the tremble of his hands.

"I thought she was dead," Casey said.

"Who is she?"

Casey leaned the shotgun beside the door and sat on the bed. He rubbed his face.

"The way it was went like this," he said. "Me and Duck Sparker were playing hide-and-seek twenty years ago. It was my turn to hunt. Duck wasn't never too hard to find because he hid in bushes, behind a tree, or in a rock hole. One time he'd been hid for a spell out Flatgap. I saw his hand hanging out of a big old log, same one you seen, I guess. It's been there since my daddy's time."

"I had me a ring whittled out of a buckeye with my initials carved on it and I thought to pull a rusty on Duck. I sneaked up to the log and put that ring on his finger. 'I take you as my wife,' I said, 'til death do us part.' Well Duck didn't say nothing and I thought he'd fell asleep while hiding. I banged that log and said, 'Wake up and kiss your husband!' The hand moved and an arm followed it out and I seen it wasn't Duck but a little dried-up woman, old as the hills. Her face was awful. She said, 'I'll wait on you.'

"I ran like a scalded pup and never told nobody, not even Duck."

Casey's voice melted into the stillness of the room. Dawn crawled above the farthest ridge and the outside air was day again. Songbirds filled the woods with sound.

"Only thing ever scared me was snakes," he said. "And I've killed my share. But I'm afraid now, Beth. Bad off afraid."

"I'll talk to Nomey this evening. You should sleep."

Casey nodded. He tucked the pistol beneath his pillow and hid the knife in the blankets. "I'll lay on the outside, Beth."

They awoke past noon, pressed tight together, and walked to her mother's. He split firewood while Beth told Nomey what had happened in the night.

"He wants to burn that log," Beth said. "Set a punk fire and smoke her out like a varmint."

Her mother's face set hard into a frown. A striped engineer's hat covered her head.

"I'd not do that," Nomey said. "She might take a notion to do the same to you. Only one woman got the power to be that mean, but I thought the buzzards had her by now."

"You act like you know her."

"Honey, I do," her mother said. "That woman fetched me into this world."

"Who?"

"The last granny-woman in these parts. She caught three hundred babies on this creek. It got close to your time, she'd be waiting in the woods. You could smell her pipe smoke. When the baby started, she'd walk right in the house with nary a word said. Just go to work. She stopped birthing after that hospital got built in Rocksalt. She got withered up like a blight hit her, and disappeared off creation. But sometimes you could smell that pipe strong, like burning cedar chips.

"People said she left her homeplace and went up Flatgap. Long time back, they quarried rock out of a cave up there and when weather pushed down, her fire smoke hung in the trees. I reckon she's still living in that cave. That log just hides the cave hole."

Dusk slipped along the creek, filtering through the trees. Beth rolled a cigarette and held the gumless flap for her mother to lick. Nomey split a wooden match, flared half to light the cigarette, tucked the other piece into her cap.

"It's unreckoning what she might do," Nomey said.

"She never did have a man or kids of her own. Best be nice by her, keep her close."

"How?"

"Two ways, and you ought to pray the first way works. Take and leave food at the mouth of that log ever so often. Not so much she'll think you're begging or buying, and not too little either. Three, four ears of corn'd be good. Don't say nothing and don't be scared. Just walk up bold and leave it."

"What's the other way?"

"A whole lot worse." She raised her voice. "Casey! You come in here."

Boots clumped and the door banged. "Chopped enough wood for a month of Sundays," he said.

"You're mine now," Nomey said, "over marrying Beth."

Casey nodded, looking at the floor.

"You listen at me on this. Stay away from Flatgap and leave them guns at the house. You hear me."

"Yes, ma'am."

"There's more to it than you think. I know you're fierce, but this takes another kind. You'll have to be stouter than you ever was. You've got to do what me and Beth tells you."

"I will."

"You swear?"

"I ain't broke my word yet."

Nomey dug in a pocket for a chunk of moly root. "Make a hole in this and wear it," she said. "Now you'uns get home."

For a year, Beth left garden vegetables by the log's

mouth. At fall slaughter she took hog; in winter, fresh venison. She missed her cycle and two months later her belly showed. When Casey came home from clearing timber, Beth's eyes were shy. "I've got a secret," she said. "I'm filled with us."

Casey's beard opened in a smile. He hugged her, then released her, frowning. "Did that hurt?"

"You can't squeeze it out that easy. It ain't no bigger than a radish."

They slept with their hands together on Beth's middle. In the morning Casey left to plow while Beth moved through the house, planning for her child. She opened the kitchen window. A breeze carried birdsong in the house, followed by the pungent scent of burnt cedar. She squeezed the moly root and prayed.

The pipe smoke smell grew stronger every day. After a week, she went to her mother's house and returned by midday. Nomey was right, the other way was worse than bad. Beth waited until the first day of the next full moon, then walked out Flatgap Ridge. Beyond it lay the massive shadow of Shawnee Rock. Beth stopped at the end of the ridge, face damp, fingers clenched. The log opening was dark as night.

"Aunt Granny Lith," Beth said. "I'm calling your name. I want my family left alone. You think we're married to the same man, but we ain't. He lives with me. I'll send him here tonight and you'll have a man for one night, not no more. You're too old to be a wife but you won't die like you were born. You got my word."

Beth stroked her swelling belly and watched a sparrow chase a jay. She turned damp leaves beneath the tree and rooted in the earth. An inch below the surface lay a chestnut with a finger-sized hole. It was brittle, nearly rotten. Beth felt the baby kick.

After supper she told Casey about the cedar smell, what Nomey had said they had to do, and the visit to the log on Flatgap Ridge. Casey finished his salad of wild ramps and cress. His voice was gentle.

"I don't know much on a woman pregnant," he said, "but I've heard it makes your mind take to spinning. Were you sick this morning?"

"You got to go up on Flatgap tonight, by yourself."

"Won't."

"You leave your clothes by the log and you crawl right inside there. It opens to an old cave."

"Ain't about to."

"Remember what Nomey said. You got to listen and do what we say. It's for the baby, your daughter."

Casey laid his fork down and straightened his back in the maple chair. His thick-knuckled hands pressed the table.

"A girl?"

"Nomey took a token on it."

"A token! I'm sick of tokens, Beth. That's all you two can do. Give a man an old piece of root and take his pistol. Go out in the woods and dicker with a log. That ain't my way, Beth. Someone crosses me, I stay crossed. I plow, hunt, and chop. I work, by God. I work!"

"Tokens work, too."

"I never seen one."

"It's knowing more than seeing."

"You ain't the only one knows things. My daddy run

animals out of the garden all his life. You can't ask a rabbit to leave your lettuce alone. You got to kill it."

Casey tore a sleeve from his shirt. He lifted a jug of kerosene and stuffed the sleeve in the narrow mouth. He grabbed a fistful of matches from the stove.

"Won't do no good," Beth said. "Even a groundhog's got two or three back doors."

"She ain't no groundhog."

"You'll just make her mad."

"We'll be square, then."

Casey lifted his shotgun and went outside. Beth heard a crash of shattering glass, then the shotgun's roar. Before the echo faded, he fired the other barrel. Ejected shells bounced against the porch. Two more blasts came and Casey stepped inside, bleeding from his forehead.

"Missed," he said.

"Was it her?"

"Biggest nighthawk I ever did see. First step off the porch, it flew at my head. I dropped the coal oil and busted it." He wiped his face and licked the blood. "Never knew a bird to act that way before."

"Come here, Casey." Her voice was low and calm. "I got something to show you."

She rolled the chestnut ring across the table. Casey picked it up carefully. Carved into the shell were his initials.

"Where'd you get this from?"

"Her."

"It ain't right, me going up there."

"You got to."

"You're my wife."

"That's why I can say."

"It's against everything."

"Not if I tell you to."

"I can't."

"It's the only way."

"That don't make it right."

"You gave your word."

Casey smashed the chestnut with his fist. He pounded the shell to tiny pieces, swept them to the floor.

"I can fix your shirt," Beth said.

"Me, too." Casey ripped the other sleeve away. "Nothing wrong with it now."

She embraced him, rocking and moaning low in her throat. At dusk he left the house. The air was white as day from the moon bloated full above the ridge. Beth watched him walk into the night, the first time she'd seen him without a gun.

She melted lye on the stove, stirred in hog tallow and crumbled sage. She ground the broken chestnut and sprinkled the powder in a pot. After it cooled, she coated the tin bottom of a washtub with the mixture and began heating water, waiting without sleep for his return.

Dawn's light angled through the trees, changing dew to ground fog rising from the hollow. Beth stiffened at a sound on the porch. Casey entered, swaying and shirtless. Nail marks gashed his shoulders and dark clots clung to his chest. He shuffled across the floor in unlaced boots.

"Don't look at me," he said.

He threw his pants outside while she poured scalding water in the washtub. Casey crouched in the steam, hugging his knees while Beth scrubbed his body raw. She helped him to bed, where he lay two weeks, chilled and quaking with fever. Nomey came to dress his wounds and fill the house with the smell of snakeroot tea. They changed the sweat-soaked sheets every morning and night.

On the fifteenth day, Casey opened calm eyes.

"Beth," he said.

"I'm here."

He slept again and Nomey left. The next day he sat wrapped in a quilt by the stove.

"Got any tobacco on you?" he said.

"You don't smoke, Casey."

"I'm starting."

She found some butts her mother had left and rolled him a fresh one. When half was gone, he spoke.

"She begged me, Beth. She flat out begged me."

"She shouldn't have."

"No, not that. After that. She begged me after."

"What?"

"To kill her."

He inhaled, watching the smoke stream into the air like water. The cigarette fell. He lowered his face to his hands and cried for a long time.

Beth tethered the mule on the creek bank, walked down to the pickup, and tumbled Casey to the ground. She used a crowbar to pry the seat loose from the truck. She tied him to the seat and hooked the logging chain to a rusty spring. At the top of the hill, she broke a willow switch and whipped the mule. Muscles rippled beneath its hide.

Each nostril puffed mist and saliva foamed from its mouth.

"Pull," Beth yelled again and again.

The mule lurched slowly forward. When the seat reached the top of the ridge, Beth wedged a shoulder under Casey's crotch, and lifted him across the animal's back. She tied his wrist to an ankle, knotting the rope tight against the mule's belly. Her clothes were damp with sweat. Casey and the animal formed a black seamless shape in the darkness of the woods. Beth led the mule down the hollow and up the creek. At the wide place where she'd first met Casey, she tossed Lil's hair into the water, and watched it swirl away.

She unloaded him onto the porch and threw a quilt over him. Casey curled on his side, tucking hands between his knees, his breath coming in ragged snorts. Beth undressed and cleaned the bruised wound on her hip. Her face was scratched and her feet ached. She lay in bed, wishing the long night all those years ago had been this easy. It had broken a part of Casey and graveled him up pretty bad. She didn't think about it often but when she did, she knew that what they'd done was right. Their four girls were proof enough, grown now, and gone.

Hours later she woke from Casey's weight on the mattress. Outside, a rooster bellowed to his hens. Casey's face poked pale and slack from the quilt.

"I lost the truck, Beth."

"You'll find it."

"But I came home," he said. "I always come home."

"Lay down now."

She scooted across the tick. Casey fumbled straps

and slid his overalls to the floor. Beth spread the quilt over them as he snuggled against her.

"Ain't never stayed a night away but the one, Beth."

"I know."

"Wished I hadn't then."

"I never think about it anymore."

"You didn't kill Lil, did you?"

"No."

"Sometimes I don't think I been much good to you."

"You're here," Beth said.

"I feel kindly rough."

"Still drunk's all. There's one good way to cure that and I don't mean coffee."

She opened her legs and towed Casey until his head lay between her breasts. She groaned as he mashed her hip.

"What's wrong, Beth?"

"Hip."

"Bad hurt?"

"No. Banged it on the corncrib or something."

"You always did hurt too easy."

She smiled at his ear, brushing her fingers along his lower back. He smelled of dirt and moonshine. She lifted her knees to guide him with her thighs.

NINE-BALL

Every afternoon Everett and his father drove to Clay Creek Grade School for barrels of leftover lunch to feed their hogs. Everett kept the heater on year-round to blow the smell out the windows. The WPA had built the grade school fifty years ago, but next summer the state was closing it.

Everett glanced at his father, who stared straight ahead, a warm beer between his legs.

"What'll we do when school shuts down?" Everett said.

"Get by, I reckon."

Everett left the blacktop for Bobcat Hollow, driving

with his head tipped to aim his good eye at the road. He slowed for an oak bridge, gray from sun and flood. Steep hills laced with rock and timber rose on both sides of the narrow hollow. At its end, their house jutted from the hillside, its front supported by columns of stacked brick. Barbed wire fenced the yard to pen the hogs. Everett backed the truck to the wooden trough, watching hogs charge across the lot, their undersides stained brown by mud.

"Ain't nothing cheaper than hogs to raise," his father said. He threw his empty beer can in the creek and walked to the house.

Everett emptied a barrel of slop over the fence. The steady stream was almost pretty, fast-flowing threads of milk specked with broccoli and corn. The boar stood at the middle of the trough while the rest fought for position, snapping their jaws and thudding heavy flanks. The smallest hog waited in the rear.

A dark strip of sky lay above the ridge and Everett wondered what he could see if hills weren't everywhere he looked. His three older brothers lived out there but never came home, wrote, or called. His father liked to say they'd all left as soon as they were weaned except the runt and the bitch—Everett and his sister. Sue hadn't really moved out, she just stopped sleeping at home.

He walked the board path to the house, where the scent of frying pork churned his stomach. For years pork had been his favorite meal. Now ham tasted the way slop smelled. He had explained this to his sister once and a grin had creased her freckles.

"Ain't nothing wrong with that," Sue said. "It's like

the time I ate violets on account of them smelling so good. Just to look at them makes me want to vomit now."

Everett nodded, awed by her wisdom in simple matters. She'd always said he was lucky to have a walleye; it allowed him to see more than other people, and she wished she'd gotten it instead of him. Everett told her he'd swap it for anything.

"Anything? she asked, unbuttoning her blouse and grinning until he blushed and turned away. He'd stayed in the woods all day, finally understanding why his brothers had left home so soon.

His father fixed the same meal every night—soup, beans, corn bread, and pork. A pint bottle of bourbon stood beside his plate. He smoked a cigarette while he ate, bread crumbs clinging to the filter. After supper Everett knew his father would finish the bottle in front of the television.

"Pool hall," Everett mumbled and pushed back from the table. His father didn't answer.

Everett sprinkled after-shave in the truck cab to cut the smell of hog. The runt snuffled through mud below the trough, searching spilled food. It looked at Everett through pale lashes. Everett leaned from the window.

"Hey, hog," he said, his voice soft. "Fuck you, hog."

He drove down the hollow to the main road, and headed for Quentin's pool hall. Five years ago, after Everett's mother died, Quentin had taught him how to play. The terrain of pool was flat and clean, and Everett could make the balls do what he wanted. There were no secrets in pool, no hidden trouble. Everything stayed visible. When he was shooting well, time moved very fast. He always played alone.

Across the pool hall's packed dirt lot sat Jesse's new red pickup with a gun rack in the rear window. Jesse worked in the coalfields two counties away, near Blue Lick River, and drove home every weekend to show off his money. He was short with big shoulders, a man who'd peaked by the eighth grade. Jesse was the only boy Sue had refused to date, and he hated Everett for it.

Movement flashed inside a black van Everett had never seen before. Someone had brought a dog, he decided, probably a valuable coonhound he was afraid to leave at home. Everett walked past Jesse's pickup, wishing his truck had a gun rack instead of garbage cans. He polished the toe of each boot on his opposite calf and pushed the heavy door open. Flies the size of bullets droned the smoky air. Lard buckets for tobacco spit sat in each corner.

A cue ball sailed off the table and smacked Jesse's thigh.

"You hurt?" someone asked.

Jesse lifted the ball in a big-knuckled hand. "Didn't hit me," he said, and laughed a short bark. He tossed the ball to a stranger. Jesse snapped a stove match against his fly and lit a cigarette, staring at Everett.

"It's a Wall Eye," Jesse said.

Everett kept walking, lips clamped like pliers. Quentin unlocked a tiny padlock, more for show than security, and removed a cue from a rack. Taped to the butt was a scrap of paper printed with Everett's name. Three other private sticks stood in the rack.

"Good wood," Quentin said.

"Just a stick."

"Could do worse."

"I have."

"You will," Quentin said. "How's your daddy?"

Everett squeezed the cue as hard as he could, knowing it would hold. He'd seen one break, but it had taken three blows across a man's back, a poor way to treat a good stick. He slowly relaxed, the cue damp in his palms.

Quentin opened a round tin of snuff and dipped a pinch, tucking it behind his lip and working it into position with his tongue. The corners of his mouth were black. He jerked his head to indicate a table.

"Boy yonder is tearing up pill-pool at two bucks a pill."

"He can keep it," Everett said.

Quentin punched his arm. "Good man, boy," he said. "Gamblers die broke."

Everett shot a rack, banking the balls around a slash in the felt. He squatted to slip another quarter in the slot, listening for his favorite sound, the dull rumble of balls. Jesse brayed from the far corner, where he played nine-ball with two strangers. Everett figured they owned the black van and the dog. They were shooting the best table, regulation size, rented by the hour instead of coin operated. Below each pocket hung a braided leather pouch. It was ideal for nine-ball, a game he'd never liked. The first eight balls were shot in numerical order and whoever made the nine ball won. Everett preferred the precision of straight pool.

Jesse moved around the table, rubbing the cue between his legs and talking loud.

"First time I had her she could piss in a thimble," he said. "Now she's got a stream wide as a handsaw."

The strangers grinned, leaning on their cues as if they were hoe handles. Quentin walked to the table and spoke quietly. The men stiffened, staring at Everett. Quentin went to the jukebox.

"Hey, Everett," he called, "name it!"

"L-8," said Everett.

Quentin pushed the button for Boxcar Willie's song about seeing the world from a slow freight train. Everett concentrated on his practice. The side pockets were the hard pockets, Quentin always said, and the long shots were the hard shots. After several racks, his arm felt limber and he was controlling the cue ball well. Jesse's high voice rose above the crack of balls.

"Can't ask much from Wall Eye no way. His daddy'd done better to raise him like a hog. Could have sold him off and got some good out of him that way."

Everett's back stiffened. He felt cold inside but his skin was hot. He crossed the room to the table and the two strangers gripped their cues across their bodies. Quentin began moving slowly from the back. Jesse pressed a finger to his nostril and blew snot to the cement floor.

"What are you looking at?" he said.

"Shoot some pool."

"Money game," sneered Jesse. "Dollar on the five and two on the nine."

"Oh," said Everett, turning away. "Thought you said money."

One of the strangers grinned. He lifted a dirty cap and pressed it back to his head. "How much you fixing to lose?"

"Ten," Everett said.

"Show it."

"He don't have to," Quentin said. "This ain't town."

"I'm not from town," the man said. "Me and my buddy work the river loading coal."

"The Blue Lick's not that close," Quentin said.

"Jesse brung us up here for some tail but I ain't seen none yet." He grinned to his friend. "Porter gets it and me and you are stuck in a damn game room. That Porter, he honks the horn every time he's finished."

Balls thundered into the trough below a table, and someone asked Quentin for change. Everett lost the coin toss and shot fourth, following Jesse. If the others played well, he'd lose before his chance to shoot, and ten dollars was all he had. The riverman ran five balls and left a lousy leave. His buddy made the eight ball without calling it.

"No slop," Jesse said. He grinned at Everett. "Call everything and keep your slop at home."

Everett tightened his grip on the cue. As long as he stayed on the other side of the table from Jesse, he'd be all right. In a fight, Jesse would come at him from the side and pound his bad eye. He'd done it twice before.

Jesse rushed his shot and missed. Everett dropped the nine with a simple combination for twenty dollars, half the money. Jesse spat between his teeth. "Forty on the nine," he said. "No splits."

Everyone nodded and Everett broke. Two balls fell and he made two more before trapping himself in a corner. Both the rivermen missed.

Jesse made the seven, but the cue ball rolled to the rail, trapped behind the nine. He could shoot a long bank on the eight, or nudge the cue ball and leave Everett the same choice. Jesse blew on his bridge hand. He lined up the shot and gently tapped the white ball.

"Dirty pool's still pool, ain't it," he said.

The riverman tucked the cue into his armpit and over his forearm like a rifle.

Everett wiped his forehead, smearing blue chalk into the sweat. If he did the same as Jesse, they would all pass until someone made a mistake and left the next man an easy shot. Never play safe, Quentin had said. Play for the game, not the shot. Always forward.

Everett bent his knees and spread his legs, head cocked sideways to keep his good eye directed down the nicked cue. He was too close to the rail, on top of the ball.

"Twenty-five bucks you miss," Jesse said.

"I want some of that," said the riverman. His friend nodded.

Everett stroked the top of the cue ball. It sped down the table, lost momentum ricocheting out of the corner, and slowed as it traveled back. It clicked the eight with just enough force to shove it in the pocket.

"I be dogged," said the riverman.

"Nice shot," his friend said.

"Lucky," Jesse muttered.

Everett exhaled as he leaned over the table for the nine ball. It dropped easily in the corner. Quentin lifted his eyebrows to the locked cue rack on the wall. Everett shook his head, fingering the old yellow tape on the stick. A rapid fiddle whined from the jukebox.

The riverman won the next game and Everett won two more. Jesse raised the bet to sixty, counting on a win to regain his losses. Play slowed at the surrounding tables as people watched. Everett broke, balls scattered, and the six crashed into a corner pocket. He called a combination on the nine. As he drew his stick to shoot, Jesse spoke in a voice cold as metal.

"I hear Wall Eye went to sows after Sue shut him off."

Everett froze, staring at the cue ball blued by chalk like a bruise. His bad eye spiraled toward the ceiling. He knew what people thought, what everyone on the creek said, but they usually hushed around him. He took a deep breath and faced the table. Shoot each shot one at a time, Quentin had said. Shut your ears off and don't listen to nobody.

Everett sighted on the ball. Two quick clicks sounded and the nine fell into the side. He leaned on his stick. Jesse lit a cigarette and flicked the burning match at Everett. A spider hopped away from it on the floor.

"You're chicken of me, ain't you, Wall Eye," Jesse said.

The riverman moved around the table to get his back against a wall. "Rack, loser," he said to Jesse. He tossed money on the table. "Pay him and rack."

Jesse jerked his wallet in front of him, jingling the silver chain that clipped it to a belt loop. He snapped his wrist to throw the money. A fifty-dollar bill drifted to the table.

"Hundred a game," Jesse said. "Who all's in?"

The riverman nodded. The other man backed from the table and leaned his stick against the wall. He bit his thumbnail, peeled it half off, and used it to pick his teeth.

"I'll play," Everett said.

He went outside and around the building to urinate against the shadowed wall. Money clogged his pockets and he wondered whose picture was on a fifty. Across the lot, the black van was rocking steadily. Everett heard a low grunt that didn't sound like a dog.

He hurried inside, where the colored balls lay in a diamond shape, waiting to be knocked apart. Nothing fell on Everett's break. Jesse and the riverman each made a shot and missed the next. Everett called a combination. The nine ball smacked into the pocket for two hundred dollars and he gathered the money, more than he'd ever seen before. The riverman racked while Jesse sandpapered the tip of his stick. It unscrewed to two pieces that fit in a vinyl case. He rubbed talcum on the burnished wood.

Everett pumped his arm and sank two on the break. He made three more, then paced around the table twice. The seven through nine were set to run with no chance for a combination. He had to make them all or lose. He dropped the seven and the eight, but the cue ball rolled too far for shape on the nine. It was a terrible leave.

"A hair hard," the riverman said. "But you can cut her."

"What're you telling him that for," Jesse said. "It's your money, too."

"Good pool's still pool."

The nine was an inch from the back rail. The cue lay in the middle of the table, aligned with the nine. If Everett shot too hard, the cue ball would carom off the table; too soft and the nine wouldn't fall in the corner. He had to shave the nine ball gently into the pocket. A miss would give Jesse the game.

Planting one foot, Everett raised the other behind him. He hitched his body forward to brace his thigh, stretching the table's length. His bridge hand was steady as a gun rest. Jesse dragged a stool from a video game and sat directly behind the nine ball.

"Double or nothing," Jesse said.

"Yup."

A car horn sounded outside, three bursts. The riverman chuckled. "That's Porter," he said. "All done."

Jesse rocked his head above the table, sucking air through his teeth. Everett knew that asking him to move would be giving in, admitting that the cheap tactic worked. Everett peered down the cue, one elbow propped on the felt-covered slate, his fingers splayed for balance. He saw the spot to hit. It was one more shot, just another shot, and he had to shoot softly, very softly.

"Which one makes more racket," Jesse said, "a hog or Sue?"

The screen door banged behind Everett, and he heard his sister's laugh.

"I do!" she said. "Damned if I don't!"

Everett hit the ball as hard as he could. It kissed the nine in the pocket, hopped high over the rail, and bounced against Jesse's face. He screamed and fell off the stool. The cue ball landed on the table.

"By God, Porter," said the riverman. "I wished you'd showed up a half hour ago. I done give a week's pay to this boy."

Sue pushed her face against Porter's chest and smiled at Everett. Lipstick tinted her front teeth. She was weaving drunk, and her jeans were unzipped. Fresh bruises marked both her arms.

"Hidy, brother," she said. "You ought to see their van."

The riverman looked at him, then quickly away. Someone whistled. Jesse scrambled from the floor, his nose streaming blood. "Table scratch, Wall Eye! You owe me a hundred bucks!"

Quentin stepped in front of Jesse. "Somebody hit you?" he said.

"Fell off the damn stool," Jesse said. "Tell that bastard he owes me money."

"He don't owe nobody nothing," said the riverman. "Look where the cue ball's at."

The nine was gone and the white ball was lying alone in the middle of the table, throwing a crescent shadow.

"That ain't no scratch," Quentin said.

"The cue ball busted me in the nose," Jesse said. "He cheated some way."

The room became very quiet. Porter pulled Sue out of range and joined the two men from the river. Players moved from the back tables, holding cues, staring at the strangers. Everett realized everyone was waiting for him to deny Jesse's accusation, but he didn't know what to say. He wasn't sure that how he'd won was fair.

The riverman threw money on the table.

"It was a clean game," he said. "That little piss-ant's looking to get hurt talking that way."

"Pay up," Quentin said to Jesse. "Or you're all done shooting here."

"I ain't got but sixty dollars." Jesse spat pink and looked at the men behind him. "I'm good for it. Who'll cover me till next week?"

No one spoke. Everett understood that they weren't backing him up, or Quentin either. It was Friday night and they didn't like Jesse. Whatever happened, they would enjoy.

"Take something off him," the riverman said. "Fancy cue stick, maybe. What size boots you wear?"

Everett shook his head. Winning no longer mattered, and he wished Sue wasn't his sister.

"You got to take something," Quentin said.

"Gun rack," Everett whispered.

Quentin jerked his head to the door. "Red pickup," he said.

The three men led Jesse outside. Quentin unplugged the jukebox and began turning off lights. "Closing time," he said.

The players left, snickering at Sue as they passed. Everett forced himself to look at her. She sagged against the table.

"Your face is all marked up with blue," she said.

"It's just chalk."

His voice echoed in the vacant room. A hand-printed sign was taped to the far wall, its yellow edges curling. NO FIGHTS, the sign read, NO GAMBLING. LADIES WELCOME. Someone had killed a bug against it.

"Need any money?" He pointed to the table. "I got plenty."

"No," she said. "I ain't about to start taking it now. Not off you anyway."

"Why not?"

"You ever see a girl in here before?"

Everett shook his head.

"Well, I'm the first, then," she said. "I'm fit for it, don't you think."

"I don't know."

"You know," she said. "Don't go playing like you don't. I'm sick of it. Sick to death of it from you and everyone else."

"Of what?"

"You know that, too."

Everett placed the cue on the table. He pushed the stick and it rolled smoothly with no bow, a good cue. He wanted to run, but couldn't; the pool hall was where he ran to. His head hurt.

"Not me," he whispered. "I never done it."

Sue stepped forward and slapped him in the face.

"No, you never did, did you! And don't go getting brigetty over it either. Many's the time you could have, but you never. You just looked at me with that old eye, like I wasn't no better than one of them hogs. Well I am, Everett. I'm here to tell you. I am!"

Everett's cheek stung and his head was throbbing. He wished he'd done it with her, too. He'd missed something that everyone knew more about than him. Now he'd never have the chance.

The riverman brought the gun rack in and set it on the pool table. The sound of Jesse's truck came through the door. Gravel scattered against the pool hall before his tires squealed on the blacktop.

Porter came inside and slipped an arm around Sue's waist.

"You coming, honey?" he said.

"Where to?"

"Wherever."

Sue stared at Everett, and Everett nodded.

"He's my brother, Porter," she said. "My best brother."

"Good pool player, too," the riverman said. "Your all's family sure grows them good."

"Only him." Sue tugged Porter's arm. "Come on, let's go to Rocksalt."

"I don't know, honey. Night like this, we might wake up in the pokey."

"I don't care," she said. "They ain't got a woman's jail and they won't put me in with men. I can do what I damn well want. I'm freer than any man I ever met."

They left the pool hall laughing. Dead gnats and ashes littered the worn felt on the table. Quentin mopped blood from the floor.

"If the cue ball goes off the table," Everett said, "when's it no good?"

"Out of play, you mean?"

Everett nodded.

"When it hits the floor," Quentin said. "Cue ball's like me—alive till it's down."

He continued mopping the pale spot in the dirty floor. Tomorrow night it would be covered with grime again. Everett had never seen the pool hall clean, just mopped in patches that never overlapped.

"What'll you take for that stick?" Everett said.

"It's yours."

"I'll pay you."

"You put more quarters in these tables than any man on the creek. Take it and hush up about it."

Everett held the cue, a standard stick like a million others, pale yellow with a brown butt. He tore away the taped paper bearing his name, crumpled it, and dropped it into a bucket. He watched the paper trying to unfold. It didn't quite make it, stuck in tobacco spit.

"I'm leaving here," he said.

"Comes a time, son. Comes a time. I stood gone nine years once."

"But you came back," Everett said.

"It ain't the same as it is here."

"I know it."

"You will," said Quentin.

Everett plugged in the jukebox and pressed L-8. Boxcar Willie told him about the Rockies, the Great Salt Lake, and the Navajo. Quentin flicked snuff at a bucket, ringing loud in the empty room. He lifted his cap and rubbed the bald rectangle on top of his head.

"Go on," he said, "if you're going to."

Everett stared at him, nodded once, and left. He strapped the gun rack in his rear window and placed the cue stick in the slots. The shadowy hills crowded the road as he drove away. At the mouth of his hollow, he stomped the brake, bounced up the dirt road, and parked beside the hog pen. He studied the fifty in the cab's dim light. It was Grant. He remembered a grade school teacher saying that Grant was a drunk. Everett stepped out of the truck and moved his hand along the fence until he found a barb. He twisted the bill around the wire, each time forcing the metal sliver through the paper. His father would find it in the morning. The picture even looked a little like him.

From the blackness of the pen came a gruff snort. If

Sue could do whatever she wanted, so could he. He un-latched the narrow gate and worked it through the mud until he made a small opening. The runt could go if it wanted to. It would probably get killed on the road, but it would die here anyway. He drove slowly out of the hollow, the pool cue rattling in the gun rack. At the black-top he headed west, trying to imagine living in a world without hills.

VINTAGE
CONTEMPORARIES

____ I Pass Like Night by Jonathan Ames	$8.95	0-679-72857-0
____ The Mezzanine by Nicholson Baker	$7.95	0-679-72576-8
____ Room Temperature by Nicholson Baker	$9.00	0-679-73440-6
____ Chilly Scenes of Winter by Ann Beattie	$9.95	0-679-73234-9
____ Distortions by Ann Beattie	$9.95	0-679-73235-7
____ Falling in Place by Ann Beattie	$10.00	0-679-73192-X
____ Love Always by Ann Beattie	$8.95	0-394-74418-7
____ Picturing Will by Ann Beattie	$9.95	0-679-73194-6
____ Secrets and Surprises by Ann Beattie	$10.00	0-679-73193-8
____ A Farm Under a Lake by Martha Bergland	$9.95	0-679-73011-7
____ Dream of the Wolf by Scott Bradfield	$10.00	0-679-73638-7
____ The History of Luminous Motion by Scott Bradfield	$8.95	0-679-72943-7
____ First Love and Other Sorrows by Harold Brodkey	$7.95	0-679-72075-8
____ The Debut by Anita Brookner	$8.95	0-679-72712-4
____ Latecomers by Anita Brookner	$8.95	0-679-72668-3
____ Lewis Percy by Anita Brookner	$10.00	0-679-72944-5
____ Big Bad Love by Larry Brown	$10.00	0-679-73491-0
____ Dirty Work by Larry Brown	$9.95	0-679-73049-4
____ Harry and Catherine by Frederick Busch	$10.00	0-679-73076-1
____ Sleeping in Flame by Jonathan Carroll	$8.95	0-679-72777-9
____ Cathedral by Raymond Carver	$8.95	0-679-72369-2
____ Fires by Raymond Carver	$9.00	0-679-72239-4
____ What We Talk About When We Talk About Love by Raymond Carver	$8.95	0-679-72305-6
____ Where I'm Calling From by Raymond Carver	$11.00	0-679-72231-9
____ The House on Mango Street by Sandra Cisneros	$9.00	0-679-73477-5
____ Woman Hollering Creek by Sandra Cisneros	$10.00	0-679-73856-8
____ I Look Divine by Christopher Coe	$5.95	0-394-75995-8
____ Dancing Bear by James Crumley	$8.95	0-394-72576-X
____ The Last Good Kiss by James Crumley	$9.95	0-394-75989-3
____ One to Count Cadence by James Crumley	$9.95	0-394-73559-5
____ The Wrong Case by James Crumley	$7.95	0-394-73558-7
____ The Wars of Heaven by Richard Currey	$9.00	0-679-73465-1
____ The Colorist by Susan Daitch	$8.95	0-679-72492-3
____ The Last Election by Pete Davies	$6.95	0-394-74702-X
____ Great Jones Street by Don DeLillo	$9.95	0-679-72303-X

**VINTAGE
CONTEMPORARIES**

___ **The Names** by Don DeLillo	$11.00	0-679-72295-5
___ **Players** by Don DeLillo	$7.95	0-679-72293-9
___ **Ratner's Star** by Don DeLillo	$8.95	0-679-72292-0
___ **Running Dog** by Don DeLillo	$7.95	0-679-72294-7
___ **The Commitments** by Roddy Doyle	$8.00	0-679-72174-6
___ **Selected Stories** by Andre Dubus	$10.95	0-679-72533-4
___ **The Coast of Chicago** by Stuart Dybek	$9.00	0-679-73334-5
___ **From Rockaway** by Jill Eisenstadt	$6.95	0-394-75761-0
___ **American Psycho** by Bret Easton Ellis	$11.00	0-679-73577-1
___ **Platitudes** by Trey Ellis	$6.95	0-394-75439-5
___ **Days Between Stations** by Steve Erickson	$6.95	0-394-74685-6
___ **Rubicon Beach** by Steve Erickson	$6.95	0-394-75513-8
___ **A Fan's Notes** by Frederick Exley	$9.95	0-679-72076-6
___ **Last Notes from Home** by Frederick Exley	$8.95	0-679-72456-7
___ **Pages from a Cold Island** by Frederick Exley	$6.95	0-394-75977-X
___ **A Piece of My Heart** by Richard Ford	$9.95	0-394-72914-5
___ **Rock Springs** by Richard Ford	$6.95	0-394-75700-9
___ **The Sportswriter** by Richard Ford	$8.95	0-394-74325-3
___ **The Ultimate Good Luck** by Richard Ford	$9.95	0-394-75089-6
___ **Wildlife** by Richard Ford	$9.00	0-679-73447-3
___ **The Chinchilla Farm** by Judith Freeman	$9.95	0-679-73052-4
___ **Bad Behavior** by Mary Gaitskill	$9.00	0-679-72327-7
___ **Fat City** by Leonard Gardner	$6.95	0-394-74316-4
___ **Ellen Foster** by Kaye Gibbons	$9.00	0-679-72866-X
___ **A Virtuous Woman** by Kaye Gibbons	$8.95	0-679-72844-9
___ **Port Tropique** by Barry Gifford	$9.00	0-679-73492-9
___ **Wild at Heart** by Barry Gifford	$8.95	0-679-73439-2
___ **The Late-Summer Passion of a Woman of Mind** by Rebecca Goldstein	$8.95	0-679-72823-6
___ **We Find Ourselves in Moontown** by Jay Gummerman	$8.95	0-679-72430-3
___ **Airships** by Barry Hannah	$5.95	0-394-72913-7
___ **The Cockroaches of Stay More** by Donald Harington	$9.95	0-679-72808-2
___ **Floating in My Mother's Palm** by Ursula Hegi	$9.00	0-679-73115-6
___ **Jack** by A.M. Homes	$8.95	0-679-73221-7
___ **The Safety of Objects** by A.M. Homes	$9.00	0-679-73629-8
___ **Saigon, Illinois** by Paul Hoover	$6.95	0-394-75849-8

VINTAGE
CONTEMPORARIES

VINTAGE CONTEMPORARIES

___ **River Dogs** by Robert Olmstead	$6.95	0-394-74684-8
___ **Soft Water** by Robert Olmstead	$6.95	0-394-75752-1
___ **Family Resemblances** by Lowry Pei	$6.95	0-394-75528-6
___ **Sirens** by Steve Pett	$9.95	0-394-75712-2
___ **Clea and Zeus Divorce** by Emily Prager	$10.00	0-394-75591-X
___ **A Visit From the Footbinder** by Emily Prager	$6.95	0-394-75592-8
___ **A Good Baby** by Leon Rooke	$10.00	0-679-72939-9
___ **Mohawk** by Richard Russo	$8.95	0-679-72577-6
___ **The Risk Pool** by Richard Russo	$8.95	0-679-72334-X
___ **The Laughing Sutra** by Mark Salzman	$10.00	0-679-73546-1
___ **Mile Zero** by Thomas Sanchez	$10.95	0-679-73260-8
___ **Rabbit Boss** by Thomas Sanchez	$8.95	0-679-72621-7
___ **Zoot-Suit Murders** by Thomas Sanchez	$10.00	0-679-73396-5
___ **Anywhere But Here** by Mona Simpson	$11.00	0-679-73738-3
___ **The Joy Luck Club** by Amy Tan	$10.00	0-679-72768-X
___ **The Player** by Michael Tolkin	$7.95	0-679-72254-8
___ **Many Things Have Happened Since He Died** by Elizabeth Dewberry Vaughn	$10.00	0-679-73568-2
___ **Myra Breckinridge and Myron** by Gore Vidal	$8.95	0-394-75444-1
___ **All It Takes** by Patricia Volk	$8.95	0-679-73044-3
___ **Birdy** by William Wharton	$10.00	0-679-73412-0
___ **Philadelphia Fire** by John Edgar Wideman	$10.00	0-679-73650-6
___ **Breaking and Entering** by Joy Williams	$6.95	0-394-75773-4
___ **Escapes** by Joy Williams	$9.00	0-679-73331-0
___ **Taking Care** by Joy Williams	$5.95	0-394-72912-9
___ **The Final Club** by Geoffrey Wolff	$11.00	0-679-73592-5
___ **Providence** by Geoffrey Wolff	$10.00	0-679-73277-2
___ **The Easter Parade** by Richard Yates	$8.95	0-679-72230-0
___ **Eleven Kinds of Loneliness** by Richard Yates	$8.95	0-679-72221-1
___ **Revolutionary Road** by Richard Yates	$8.95	0-679-72191-6

Available at your bookstore or call toll-free to order: 1-800-733-3000.
Credit cards only. Prices subject to change.

Also available from Vintage Contemporaries

• •

Picturing Will
by Ann Beattie

An absorbing novel of a curious five-year-old and the adults who surround him.

"Beattie's best novel since *Chilly Scenes of Winter* ... its depth and movement are a revelation."   —*The New York Times Book Review*

0-679-73194-6/$9.95

Where I'm Calling From
by Raymond Carver

The summation of a triumphant career from "one of the great short story writers of our time—of any time" *(Philadelphia Inquirer)*.

0-679-72231-9/$11.00

The House on Mango Street
by Sandra Cisneros

Told in a series of vignettes stunning for their eloquence, the story of a young girl growing up in the Hispanic quarter of Chicago.

"Cisneros is one of the most brilliant of today's young writers. Her work is sensitive, alert, nuanceful ... rich with music and picture."   —Gwendolyn Brooks

0-679-73477-5/$9.00

Wildlife
by Richard Ford

Set in Great Falls, Montana, an absorbing novel of a family tested to the breaking point.

"Ford brings the early Hemingway to mind. Not many writers can survive the comparison. Ford can. *Wildlife* has a look of permanence about it."   —*Newsweek*

0-679-73447-3/$9.00

The Chosen Place, the Timeless People
by Paule Marshall

A novel set on a devastated part of a Caribbean island, whose tense relationships—between natives and foreigners, blacks and whites, haves and have-nots—keenly dramatize the vicissitudes of power.

"Unforgettable ... monumental."   —*Washington Post Book World*

0-394-72633-2/$13.00

Bright Lights, Big City
by Jay McInerney

Living in Manhattan as if he owned it, a young man tries to outstrip the approach of dawn with nothing but his wit, good will and controlled substances in this celebrated novel.

"A dazzling debut, smart, heartfelt, and very, very funny."   —Tobias Wolff

0-394-72641-3/$9.00

Mama Day
by Gloria Naylor

This magical tale of a Georgia sea island centers around a powerful and loving matriarch who can call up lightning storms and see secrets in her dreams.

"This is a wonderful novel, full of spirit and sass and wisdom."   —*Washington Post*

0-679-72181-9/$10.00

Anywhere But Here
by Mona Simpson

An extraordinary novel that is at once a portrait of a mother and daughter and a brilliant exploration of the perennial urge to keep moving.

"Mona Simpson takes on—and reinvents—many of America's essential myths ... stunning."   —*The New York Times*

0-679-73738-3/$11.00

The Joy Luck Club
by Amy Tan

"Vivid ... wondrous ... what it is to be American, and a woman, mother, daughter, lover, wife, sister and friend—these are the troubling, loving alliances and affiliations that Tan molds into this remarkable novel."   —*San Francisco Chronicle*

"A jewel of a book."   —*The New York Times Book Review*

0-679-72768-X/$10.00

Philadelphia Fire
by John Edgar Wideman

"Reminiscent of Ralph Ellison's *Invisible Man*" *(Time)*, this powerful novel is based on the 1985 bombing by police of a West Philadelphia row house owned by the Afro-centric cult, Move.

"A book brimming over with brutal, emotional honesty and moments of beautiful prose lyricism."   —Charles Johnson, *Washington Post Book World*

0-679-73650-6/$10.00

• •

Available at your local bookstore,
or call toll-free to order: 1-800-733-3000
(credit cards only). Prices subject to change.

**VINTAGE
CONTEMPORARIES**